I0527560

PARSE GALAXY BOOK 8

FALLOUT STRIKE

KATE SHEERAN SWED

Copyright © 2024 by Kate Sheeran Swed

All rights reserved.

No part of this book may be reproduced in any form or by any electronic or mechanical means, including information storage and retrieval systems, without written permission from the author, except for the use of brief quotations in a book review.

This book is a work of fiction. Any resemblance to actual events or persons, living or dead, is coincidental.

Cover by Deranged Doctor Design

JOIN THE CREW!

Sign up for my newsletter and keep reading with your free VIP Crew Library Collection! It's packed full of extras from the *Parse Galaxy*, the *League of Independent Operatives*, and *The Interstellar Trials*—with bonus stories, novellas, deleted scenes, and more!

Join now at KateSheeranSwed.com/Join-The-Crew

CHAPTER 1

THE GALAXY MIGHT BE CHANGING at the pace of a shooting star, with alliances crumbling and shifting and turning from sweet to sour overnight, but Sloane was pretty sure that Shard would remain Shard until the last molecule of oxygen evaporated from its poorly generated atmosphere. And probably well after that.

As she stepped around one of the green-tinted puddles that defined the makeshift city, it was difficult to deny that there were some things in the galaxy that could use a good hard reboot. She didn't want to think about whether the cracked-off chunk of long-dead planet was even big enough to whip up its own weather systems, or where the puddles had come from if it wasn't.

Brighton stepped over her puddle's twin with a more delicate hop than she'd have imagined possible for the big man, grimacing like he could imagine all too well what was making the puddle green and was afraid it would eat right through his boots if he lingered even a beat too long.

Sloane was aware that she was fixating on the puddles. But it was easier than obsessing about the reason they were on Shard in the first place. Or at least, it kept her blood pressure at a more reasonable level.

"Hey, Brighton," she said. "This was where you joined the crew."

Brighton grunted. "After being locked in your cargo bay for several weeks."

Psh. It'd been days, at most. "Yes, well, you were a legal bounty."

Even though she'd been the one to broach the subject, Sloane didn't really want to think about it, either. Not so much because she regretted having brought Brighton onto the crew—a gut decision that'd paid off tenfold—but because the last time she'd been here, she'd walked the streets with Hilda at her side.

Now, Hilda lay unconscious in a hospital bed on *Sabre*, fighting for her life after getting shot by some Cosmic Trade Federation asshole. Maybe even dying, because of a tangle of politics that Sloane had gotten her into. With, she had to admit, a little help from her uncle.

But she could have bowed out at any time. Instead, she'd played the hero.

Well, first she'd played the selfish bounty hunter, then the runaway. *Now* she was playing the hero. But still, her crew was paying the price. Some captain she'd turned out to be. Alex was kidnapped, Ivy back on the ship monitoring her inlays for secret messages from her. Damian was gone, maybe forever.

Gareth was all right, at least, but she didn't dare risk bringing him to Shard, where a good ninety percent of the population were criminals. More likely to shoot at him or run from him than anything else. Or try to trip him, at the very least. Besides, he had his own mission.

So it was just her and Brighton.

"Are you sure about this?" the big man asked, wrinkling his

nose as they sidled past the ragged buildings. Smelling the same background rot as she, no doubt. What a place.

Sloane gave him her best and brightest fake smile. "Not even a little bit. You know where we're going?"

Brighton's gaze skipped up over the haphazard row of buildings that slumped to their right like sullen teenagers, up toward the passing hov-train she'd once attached him to in a bid to escape the Fleet. Which, despite Brighton's grousing, had worked extremely well. Good times.

The station entrance was off to their left, if a rusty set of stairs counted as an entrance. Bolts lashed it to the corner of the building at alarmingly paranoid intervals, like whoever'd put it together had been deeply uncertain of their own abilities to keep it standing.

"Yeah," Brighton said, sounding resigned. "I know where we're going."

Because despite everything, a fistful of tokens still bought information from the right people—or the wrong ones, depending on how you defined those things—and the criminal types who lived their lives slithering through the Parse Galaxy's underworld still thought they were immune to the changes that'd been roaring through the rest of the galaxy. Still thought Striker's little galactic empire bid couldn't touch them, because nothing touched them. Nothing wanted to.

And she was here to convince them otherwise.

"I don't know how you expect to get up there, though," Brighton said, and Sloane followed his gaze to a thin stick of a building in the distance, one that her brain had dismissed as a janky communications tower. It was maybe a mile off, and it stood out against the brownish-gray sky like a cavity-ridden fang. Or a needle that'd been run over by a vindictive bus, then left to rust in one of Shard's suspicious puddles.

"When you said it was a floating game, I thought you meant it moves around," she said.

"It does," Brighton said. "And it's also literally floating."

Sloane shook her head. "I suppose I can appreciate a good pun. Or at least, a solid attempt. I assume the hov-train doesn't stop there?"

Brighton grunted again. "Hov-train barely clears it. Part of the attraction."

Criminal masterminds loved a good solid brush with danger, as long as it was more the feeling than actual danger. With no authorities to chase after them on Shard, they found their thrills elsewhere. It comforted her, in a way. More evidence that they were exactly the types she was hoping to find.

"Perfect," she said. "Up to the platform we go." She started up the rickety staircase to the hov-train platform, trying not to feel uneasy about how deeply it vibrated as she stepped on it.

"Clean out your ears." Brighton put a hand on her arm, holding her back before she could take the second step. "I said the train doesn't stop there."

For an ex-criminal, he was charmingly attached to the obvious answers. Sloane patted his cheek, then pulled her arm gently out of his grip. "Doesn't need to stop, Sunshine," she said. "Let's go."

Brighton groaned, either because he understood her plan—which would be impressive since she only half understood it herself—or because he didn't know where this was going and that made him nervous. He really ought to trust her by now.

The plan would evolve. It always did.

After a few seconds, during which she ascended several more steps, the staircase shuddered as he joined her on the way up.

And up. And up. Endlessly up, actually. She tried to imagine an inebriated criminal type making their way home by way of this staircase at the end of a long day of pickpocketing. Not a pretty thought.

"You'd think there'd be an elevator," she said after the third landing, breathing hard. She really needed to invest in some cardio equipment when this was all over.

"There is an elevator."

She shot a glance back at her security officer, expecting him to add that it was broken or something. But he just kept plodding up the steps, as if this was a stroll through Ikor's Cyber Gardens rather than a workout. "And you didn't think to mention that?"

"You didn't ask. You just went barreling up."

Sloane briefly contemplated heading back down the stairs to find the elevator, but they'd almost made it halfway to the platform. It was a matter of pride, at this point. Besides, there was someone climbing behind them now, a slim figure with their nose buried in the raised collar of a dark brown jacket. She'd only snag their suspicion if she hitched a U-turn and headed down now.

Though it might be a good way to find out if they were following her. Always a possibility.

By the time she and Brighton reached the hov-train platform, Sloane was sweating and much grumpier than she'd been when they started. The landing she'd taken for the halfway point had, in fact, been a quarter-of-the-way point; the stairs had twisted around the side of the building before jutting precariously out on their own.

That last lap had been for steel nerves only.

Brighton emerged from the stairs, looking none the worse for the climb. In fact, the corners of his mouth were twitching ever so slightly. Like he was *enjoying* this.

Or maybe he was just enjoying her suffering. Hard to tell.

Sloane watched as their popped-collar traveler friend sidled along to the end of the platform. The person seemed to be trying to avoid her notice, but that was pretty much to be expected on Shard. She'd have been more suspicious if they tried to act casual. Still, she made sure to keep them in her peripheral vision. She'd been jumped on enough hov-trains to want to avoid repeating the experience.

Her life had definitely veered into 'weird' territory. The realization that kept on realizing.

The hov-train snaked toward the station in the distance, like a flying snake keeping watch over the haphazardly arranged city below. Sloane took the opportunity to catch her breath, craning her neck in the other direction so she could study the needle-like tower.

"So the game's at the top," she said.

Brighton shrugged.

"Not the time for uncertainty, Brighton." If they had to climb back down these stairs, he was going to have to carry her.

"It's a *floating* game," he said. "It moves. Which means the intel's only good as long as no one's paying my contact enough to tip them off about someone asking around."

Sloane wiped her forehead with the back of her hand. "I thought you trusted this guy."

"I trust him as much as I trust anyone on Shard. Or the Bone System, for that matter."

Which probably wasn't very much. She should remember that, given that she was about to try negotiating with some of the System's least trustworthy citizens.

Sloane retreated half a step from the edge of the platform as the train sighed to a stop. The cars were splashed with speckles of rust, giving them a slightly diseased look. "Let's crash a card game," she said.

Brighton hesitated, his left foot poised to step into the train car. "Literally?"

Sloane grinned. "Can't leave all the good puns to the criminals."

"The quality is debatable," he grumbled. But he followed her onto the train without further complaint, so he must trust her at least a little.

Holding on to a pole and trying hard not to think about why it might be sticky, Sloane directed her gaze out the window, focusing on the jagged tower.

She wouldn't have seen the platform if she hadn't been looking for it. Bobbing casually beside the tower, it looked like one of those drink holders that were supposed to be able to float next to you in a pool. A good idea in theory, but always destined to get knocked over. The platform even sported an umbrella-like top—perhaps to protect against the wind from the train—though it reflected the brownish-red color of Shard's pitiful atmosphere instead of the cheerful colors she'd expect to see at the pool. Invisibility was the goal, rather than cheer.

As she watched, the platform dipped slightly, as if in response to a gentle wave. "How're they doing that?" she asked.

Brighton snorted. "Hijacked gravity anchors. Your favorite trick."

"Is not." He raised an eyebrow at her, and she shrugged. "Okay, I'll admit it's in the top ten."

Brighton pointed a thick finger toward the platform. "They force every other coin into reverse, and that balances the platform. Half allowing it to float, half pulling it back."

Sloane frowned at the platform, which was growing closer. "But the hov-trains on Shard are connected to the gravity channels. They'd be affected."

He gave her a wry look. "Not anymore, they're not. They fixed that little loophole after your stunt."

Must have been an expensive fix. "I'm surprised they cared."

"Are you kidding? I can think of three heists a person could run using gravity anchors and interlinked hov-trains, just off the top of my head. If there's one thing the Bone System bosses care about, it's the bottom line."

"So you're saying I'm responsible for improved infrastructure on Shard."

"Sure. And a regular meeting opportunity for the most dangerous criminal masterminds in the galaxy. These guys are supposed to hate each other."

She waved his concern away. First off, if criminal masterminds wanted to meet, then they'd find a way to meet, grav anchors or no. And second, what was wrong with a little card game among criminal bosses? It was probably keeping them out of worse trouble. Right?

She had a niggling suspicion that she sounded a little like Gareth right now. Though even he probably wouldn't be so naïve about criminal bosses meeting regularly.

The platform bobbed closer, and Sloane positioned herself beside the door, ready to hit the emergency button. "When I say go—"

"Stop right there."

She'd been so distracted by Shard's gravity engineering that she'd forgotten to watch the person who'd entered the car with them. Now, the guy stepped between her and the doors, a bright blue badge glimmering in the center of his palm. He stood a good head shorter than she, and the set of his shoulders said he was pissed about it. Or about something. A splash of thinning dark hair clung to his head like a kind of wiry moss.

"I didn't know Shard had cops." She glanced easily over his head to keep an eye on the quickly approaching tower. The train was set to pull a wide curve before presumably skimming to a stop at the top. A wide curve that would take them directly over the floating card game.

"I'm a Transport Integrity Officer," the guy said, jabbing a finger at Sloane's shoulder. "And you are responsible for two major hov-train disasters."

"Only two?" Sloane frowned. "I feel like there were more than that."

"There was the arena escape," Brighton said, holding up one finger, then adding a second. "And then the thing with Damian."

"The second one was the CTF's fault. Surely a good Transport Integrity Officer wouldn't blame *us* for the Federation's attack."

Brighton tapped his bottom lip with his finger. "Maybe for the blown-out doors, though."

"That was Damian. And we were escaping certain death."

Probable death, anyway.

"We flagged your ship when it landed on Shard," the officer blustered, cheeks flushing with annoyance. "You're banned from using the hov-train networks. You should have received a notice."

Too late for that, clearly. "Huh," she said. "Transport cops noticed us before the criminals did."

"Maybe not by much," Brighton said darkly.

The transport officer stiffened, gracing him with another sliver of height. "If you're suggesting that Transport Integrity Officers are susceptible to bribes, I'll have you know that we operate under the strictest moral guidelines. We—"

"Sorry to interrupt," Sloane said, "but our stop's coming up."

The officer paused with his mouth open. "There's no stop for at least ten minutes."

Sloane patted him on the shoulder, then stepped aside. "So innocent. Brighton? If you will?"

In one smooth motion, Brighton lifted the man up by his elbows and spun, moving the officer back to the center of the car.

Sloane pounded the emergency button, and the doors relaxed, allowing her to wrench them apart. "I'm sorry," she said, pausing with one hand on the open door. She had to raise her voice against the wind that came whipping through the car. "It's just that we're trying to save the galaxy."

And with that, she lined up her jump and leapt out of the train.

CHAPTER 2

SLOANE WAS WELL aware of her tendency to rely on plans that combined semi-calculated risks with a healthy dose of luck. To leap out of a stalled hov-train without a parachute and trust the air currents not to whip her away from her target when they seemed just as inclined to impale her on the needle-like tower as to drop her into the card game... that was the kind of gamble that yielded either a big payoff or a big catastrophe. No in between.

And yet somehow, she hadn't questioned the wisdom of the approach until she was actually falling.

Thankfully—no, *luckily*—the short drop meant there wasn't long to contemplate potential catastrophes before her feet slammed into the umbrella. Her heels punctured the fabric with an audible *rip*, and the rest of her body rushed to widen the hole as she fell straight through it. Her shoulders only held her up for a brief instant before she tumbled, ass-first, onto a round table that was strewn with cards.

Well. She *had* said she wanted to crash the game.

When she raised her head, giving it a shake to dispel the rattle of the fall, there were seven players staring at her with equally shocked expressions on their faces, their jaws dropped wide enough to surround her in a cloud of gin-and-bitter smells, eyebrows high enough to catch the next hov-train. Or hail a sky-taxi, if Shard had any of those. Two women, five men, and a dog the size of a breadbox, with pointy ears and curly gray fur that obscured its eyes. As soon as she landed, the animal started barking furiously, straining at the edge of the leash that its owner had secured to the back of his chair. Who the hell brought a dog to a floating card game?

She didn't know who was who, she realized. It felt like showing up on the day of a test having studied the wrong chapter. Or no chapter at all. Callow Clan, Fox Clan, the Mechics. Who else? Brighton would know. Where the hell was he?

Smart enough not to leap out of a moving hov-train, perhaps.

After a beat, the dog's owner threw down his cards, revealing what he'd probably thought was a winning hand. And she'd prevented him from playing it. Not the most auspicious way to introduce herself. Though it did tell her a little something about his priorities, if he was still worried about who would win the game.

"No worries," she said, trying to disguise the breathlessness in her voice. Her tailbone was still twinging from the fall. "That one had a higher card."

She pointed at one of the two women at the table, a brunette with a sharp chin and pointed ears that suggested an affiliation with the Wringers. The woman placed her cards on the table calmly, keeping them facedown. As if the game had a chance of continuing after this. Sloane tentatively pegged her as an overly optimistic type.

Sloane pushed to her feet, ignoring the protest in her lower back and hoping she hadn't cracked anything important, like a vertebra. "Hey," she said. "Heard there was a party going on. My invite got lost in the Currents, I think."

The first player to recover—by snapping his own mouth shut

and tossing his cards aside—was a thickset guy with gray hair and a jaw line wide enough to double as a shield. When he pushed his chair back from the table and stood, he was almost as tall as she was, even with the added on-the-table height. That likely made him a Mechic, with some kind of reinforced cybernetic implants that let him increase his height. Though Fox Clan liked their implants, too.

Either way, the guy was big. Sloane glanced up, hoping Brighton planned to join her before this guy tried to crush her skull between his thumb and forefinger. But though the hov-train was still stalled above, her security officer wasn't anywhere in sight. Had the Transport Integrity Officer gotten the better of him? Hard to picture how that little guy could've overtaken Brighton.

"Sloane Tarnish," the big card player said. "You've interrupted our game."

Sloane crossed her arms, mostly because they felt like dead weights at her sides. Rogue bounty hunters turned would-be galactic saviors weren't supposed to fidget. "From what I hear, you only have this game because of me."

"Don't give yourself so much credit." That was the Wringer woman, who spoke with a drawling accent that Sloane couldn't place.

Sloane studied the woman, letting her gaze linger on the prosthetic ears. "And here I thought you Wringers prided yourselves on staying on the right side of the law. I met some of your friends near Olton Moon."

She scoffed. "We're business people. We pride ourselves on taking advantage of opportunities when they arise."

With that, the woman lunged, faster than Sloane would have expected. She grabbed Sloane's ankle, moving with an almost unnatural swiftness to yank her forward. Sloane flailed, but there was nothing to grab, and nothing to keep her ass from hitting the table a second time, prompting a particularly undignified *oof* out from between her lips.

No time to dwell on the humiliation of that moment. Everyone was reaching for her now, manicured fingernails bumping up against calloused hands that looked like they'd strangled more than one impertinent bounty hunter in their day. Sloane scrambled back, weighing the possibility of climbing the now-leaning umbrella fixture. But where she'd go after that, she had no idea.

So she did the one thing she could think of: she dove *off* the table, aiming for the sliver of space between the thickset guy and the bald companion to his left.

Essentially, she threw herself at the dog.

The bald guy yelped, but it was too late. She wrapped her arms around the dog, hauling it up off the floor and into her arms. It was heavier than it looked, solid through the middle, and very soft. Made her want to bury her face in its fur. She'd have wagered the thing smelled better than any of the card players.

Clutching the dog to her chest, Sloane backed toward the edge of the platform. Which was much closer than she'd realized. They played their game in tight quarters, that was for sure.

To the dog's credit, it started licking her chin.

The bald guy threw his hands out to the sides, preventing any of his companions from making another move on her. Sloane would never do anything to hurt a dog, but the bald guy didn't know that. He could assume whatever he wanted.

"What do you want?" the bald guy asked. "Why did you come here?"

"I just want to talk." The dog was blocking her view, a little, as it tried to scramble toward her face for continued licking. Not the most dignified way to begin a negotiation. "I want us to work together."

Silence, except for the jangling of the dog's collar as it wriggled in her arms. Then the thickset guy started to laugh. "Why would we want to work with *you*?"

Sloane decided not to feel insulted by that. At least, not very. "Oh, I don't know," she said. "Something about Striker and the Cosmic Trade Federation trying to take over the entire freaking galaxy?"

"The Bone System is untouchable." The dog's owner was watching his pet, clearly still afraid she might hurt the creature. Or maybe a bit betrayed at its friendliness toward her. "Nothing has changed here."

Except a fixed up grav-anchor system, and Transit Integrity Officers who actually showed up to enforce their rules on Shard. That was pretty weird, in and of itself.

"It won't last," she said. "Striker wants all the resources in the galaxy, and that means the Bone System, too. If anything, he'll come here first. All that untapped potential you recognized? He'll see it, too."

The Wringer woman shifted her feet. The rest of them didn't move, but Sloane could feel them *intentionally* not moving. They might as well have traded meaningful glances. She'd bet her best boots that they'd discussed this very topic. And she really liked those boots.

"How long will it take Striker to shut down this little card game?" she asked. "He won't want you meeting up. Getting friendly. Maybe even joining forces."

Now they did shuffle their feet. And it might have been the wind—it *was* breezy up here—but she thought she heard some murmurs, too. They could pretend all they wanted, but they *were* worried.

The thickset guy, though, he was the one to watch. He didn't look away from her. He didn't shuffle his feet, and he definitely didn't murmur. He held her gaze, eyes boring into her with obvious malice. But it was the upward curl of his mouth that worried her the most, and the spark of humor it ignited in his expression.

In Sloane's experience, looks like that usually produced results along the lines of 'I know something you don't know.'

If nothing else, she'd learned one thing: this guy was the leader here. The head mastermind. The one they all deferred to, even if they'd never admit it out loud. Good to know.

"Striker ignores us," he said finally. "I'm more worried about how long it will take the Fleet to shut us down."

Like the Fleet cared. As long as Adu kept its business in Adu, the Fleet would stay out of it. Problem was, criminals never wanted to just keep to themselves.

"I don't know," Sloane said. "Maybe they'll be willing to let it slide."

The leader guy snorted, trading a glance with the Wringer woman over the dog-owner's head. Sloane might not know their names, but she was starting to get a feel for the hierarchy. "We know the rumors," Leader Guy said. "You're in their thrall. Just a little Fleet puppet, come to exact your own control."

Sloane wasn't sure she'd ever seen someone so committed to turning his face into a stereotypical sneer. It was like someone else was yanking on that lip of his. And his nostrils flared so hard that it looked like they were about to flip inside out.

"We all need to work together on this," she said. "All of us. I'm not here on the Fleet's behalf. I'm here on the galaxy's behalf."

"Oh? And who appointed you?"

The dog wriggled in her arms, and she patted its head, trying to keep it from slobbering on her. More than it already had. "I appointed myself, because I figured you'd see reason. Step in and help us take down the CTF."

"And end up in a Fleet prison for our trouble? Not likely."

The Wringer woman was nodding emphatically, the others

joining in a beat later. Less like a meeting of dangerous bosses than a flock of bobble-headed birds.

Only the bald guy was still looking back and forth between her and the Boss of Bosses, a clear spark of anxiety in his eyes. "Mr. Brennan," he said, "she's got my dog."

A name. Finally. Sloane almost thanked the guy out loud. Probably not good politics, though.

Brennan edged toward his bald friend, as if he thought he could defy physics and sneak around the dog owner's chair to where Sloane was standing. "May well be," he said, "that the Commander will do anything to get her back. If she's a hostage."

See, that hadn't occurred to her. Maybe the hov-train leap wasn't the worst of the risks today. She didn't like the gleam of greed in his eyes. And she really didn't like the way it reflected in the others' eyes, too.

Or at least, most of them.

"My *dog*," the bald guy said. "Horace, please."

"I don't care about your dog, Trip," Horace Brennan said. What a name. He raised a hand, and Sloane expected him to smack Trip, maybe knock him off the platform.

She was so busy wondering how they were going to navigate the tight space that she didn't hear the whining motor of the hov-tile until the board smashed into her from behind. She staggered belly-first into the table, the dog scrabbling up onto the surface to avoid getting squashed.

Of course they had guards watching the game. They'd probably each brought an entire entourage to watch their backs. She should have thought of that.

Sloane pushed back from the edge of the table and slipped the dog's leash off of its collar before shoving the animal into Trip's arms. The rest of the players were retreating to the other side of the platform, making it tilt precariously. No doubt tallying up their part of whatever billion token ransom they planned to place on her release as they watched their guards close in.

The one who'd hit Sloane made a grab for her legs, but she kicked him in the nose, and he stumbled back, tripping over a chair and flailing to keep from plummeting off the platform. NOt much room to maneuver up here.

Thankfully, Sloane caught the whine of the second hov-tile before its rider could get close enough to grab her. He swerved toward her, arms outstretched, but Sloane threw the leash up and over, catching him around the ankles.

And then she pulled.

The guard lost his balance, tumbling off his tile and onto the table. Working fast, she untangled the leash and slung it over the now-empty hov-tile, throwing her body sideways to tell it to race away from the game. Right now.

Which wasn't easy when she was hanging off the bottom instead of guiding the tile with her feet. But she worked with what she had. The tile lurched, but it lurched in the right direction, and she zoomed away from the game to the tune of the dog's barking, her legs dangling over Shard's jagged skyline.

She was just trying to figure out how to swing herself all the way up onto the tile so she could ride it properly before more guards came after her when the sweet melody of *Moneymaker*'s engines hummed in the distance. And then the ship was there, matching the hov-tile's speed from above and giving it the trippy illusion that the ship was hovering in midair.

The gangplank shuddered open, and she threw her legs sideways to yank the tile inside. Where she promptly landed in a heap in the middle of the cargo hold.

"That didn't go well!" BRO said. "That didn't go well at all! Shall I head for the Current? Brighton's letting me drive!"

"Fly," Brighton's voice chimed in. He'd gone back to the ship.

That was a good move. Though she'd love to know how he'd done it so quickly.

"Right!"

Sloane blinked, pulling herself up to sit. There was dog hair all over her shirt. And in her mouth. She rolled her tongue, spitting to try and get it out, then shook her head. Her back was sore, and her ego felt even worse. No, that hadn't gone well. It hadn't gone well at all.

When she picked herself up off the ground, she found herself looking straight into the very angry eyes of the Transport Integrity Officer who'd tried to stop her on the train. His hands were tied together, his arms looped over a pipe in the corner, and he was staring at her with murder in his eyes.

"Um, Brighton?" she said.

"Oh, right." The big man hurried down the steps to the cargo hold, shaking the whole staircase as he ran. "Not to the Current yet, BRO. Gotta drop our passenger off at his office."

Sloane got to her feet, brushing the hair off her shirt. "I'm never going to be allowed on another hov-train again."

CHAPTER 3

GARETH HADN'T THOUGHT he'd ever return here.

The destroyed water hauler he'd encountered all those weeks ago was still locked in its eerie stasis field. It *was* still eerie, despite the familiarity he'd gained with the technology that froze the wreck in place in a way that shouldn't be possible in the middle of interstellar space. Repeated dives into the fields—both intentional and otherwise—had certainly made him an unwilling expert. Even so, it just felt wrong.

A wreck like this should float, drift, move. It shouldn't stand in place like a VR module come to life.

Since his first visit here, he'd been to the asteroid mines that'd been this ship's destination, found the CTF-designed disaster there. He'd walked into Striker's trap on Cappel, hiked across Olton Moon, been imprisoned at the Hold, infiltrated Obsidian City. And still, the wrecked hauler was exactly as he'd left it. Trapped in the moment of its destruction.

Which should teach them a lot, assuming they could figure out exactly what it was they were looking for.

And that was why he was currently entering the frozen ship, which he and a small company of soldiers had been able to access by coating their armor in a layer of jaevin, the only material they'd found so far that would let them cut through a stasis field. This particular field ran straight up to the hull of the ship and then stopped, a fact they'd learned not ten minutes ago when they made their way through the unnatural stillness to cut their way onto the destroyed hauler.

All the while, his brain did its best to shuffle the field's whispers into the background. Not the easiest task.

"I look like a gaudy figurine in my grandma's collection." Ensign Sands pointed to his armor's jaevin-coated elbow, a wide gesture in his atmo suit. In the near-hour it'd taken them to reach the hauler's hull, Sands had already covered his dissatisfaction with the size of their team, the fact that he'd been asked to join the team at all, and the headaches that came along with the whispers.

Now, apparently, he objected to the jaevin. Sure, it looked a little ridiculous. But it did the job.

"I didn't realize you'd joined up for the aesthetics." Gareth turned a circle, taking in the layout of the corridor. It looked as if it'd been crushed within a giant fist, parts of the hull crumpled like a ball of paper. The stars winked through frequent holes where the hull had stressed to breaking, their light strange and dappled through the filter of the stasis field. "Maybe I should reassign you to our clothing design department."

"*Is* there a clothing design department?" Captain Pitorski sounded ready to second that reassignment. She'd taken up a spot behind Gareth and Sands, clearly organizing her team so they'd be ready to protect the only two known people in the galaxy who could communicate directly with stasis fields and Currents.

Given the choice, Gareth would have chosen a partner-in-weirdness other than Sands. But it was what it was. He and Sands had both been exposed to this specific stasis field, and it was the only variable they'd come up with so far to explain the connection—which, in addition to allowing them to hear the whispers, was also making them both sick. Gareth more than Sands, but the ensign had been battling headaches for weeks.

"I'll create one for his sake," Gareth said.

"I'd take that gig if it got me off this one." Sands held both his arms out. "I look like a Balchal's Feast decoration gone wrong. I look like the statue your neighbor buys when he comes into more money than he knows what to do with. It's just *wrong*."

As if they weren't all covered in the same stuff. Gareth ignored the ensign's complaining, studying the corridor instead. Silently cataloguing the uneven dents in the walls, the gnarled metal and scars left behind by whatever had shot them out of the vacuum.

"I thought Sloane said you were pleasant," he said.

Sands grunted. "Maybe 'pleasant' means something different to her than it does to you."

"Add a 'sir' to that, soldier," Pitorski said.

Gareth shot her a glance. "*That's* the objectionable part of what he said?"

Pitorski shrugged, but he could make out a grin behind the reflective material of her visor. "He's got a point, sir. She does like *you*."

"I see how it is, Captain," Gareth said. "Lead us on, then."

Pitorski took point, waving two soldiers to the back to cover the rear, though Gareth seriously doubted there was anything left here to attack them. Surely *Sabre*'s scanners would have noted any life signs. "Speak up if you see anything," Pitorski said. "We'll head for the bridge."

"And turn up your sensors." That was Chief Escher, her voice tinny and commanding through the comm link in his helmet. "The readings plummeted once you were out of the field."

In addition to searching for any last recordings or logs that might explain exactly what'd happened to the ship—and what kind of weapon the CTF had used against it—they were here to run tests on the field itself and to see whether they could detect any differences between this field and the others they'd collected samples of. Escher was taking the readings from *Sabre*'s lab, and they'd already received a fair number of brusque instructions from her, each of which involved stopping or swerving or swinging their sensors closer to a particular object or pocket of space.

"Getting anything?" Gareth asked.

"There's something here all right, though it'd be easier with *Moneymaker*'s lab," she said. "Alex's equipment is more sensitive."

"Than Fleet equipment?" Pitorski asked.

"Ten times more sensitive." Escher sighed. "But we work with what we've got."

Two weeks ago, Escher had been fighting to remain on *Sabre*, claiming its materials had to be superior. Times changed.

But it was difficult to be amused by that when the lab's owner had gone missing. And when he was surrounded by the tomb of an unarmed ship, destroyed without apparent reason or warning. The hauler hadn't even had any guns, or a way to defend itself. It shouldn't have needed to.

"*Moneymaker* will be back from Adu soon," Gareth said. "Then you can use the lab all you want, assuming Sloane signs off on the plan."

He doubted she'd protest, but it was good to set expectations up front. Her ship, her rules.

"Commander," Sands said, waving him over to a particularly large hole in the hull, where one of the seams had been wrenched apart by an enormously strong force. Gareth joined him, keeping one hand on the interior wall, blinking away the disorientation that came with looking straight out into space. Stars winking through the stasis field, sending a symphony of glittering light bouncing through a graveyard of metallic slivers and other detritus that'd exploded out of the ship only to be caught in stasis.

Gareth supposed Escher and her team would be able to pinpoint exactly when the stasis field had been activated, down to the millisecond, based on the position of the shrapnel alone.

From here, it was unnerving enough to make his stomach turn a somersault. He was used to looking out into the void, but not like this. The stars should be solid and unblinking; the black should be clear.

"The hull wasn't punctured from the outside," Sands said, calling Gareth's thoughts back to the ruptured hull. "It was blown *out*. Look."

Gareth followed the ensign's attention to the edge of the hole, where the metal bent and curled toward the vacuum. Not consistent with a strike from outside. "Sabotage?"

Maybe a CTF operative had sneaked on board. But why? Why take out a water hauler, from the inside *or* the outside, and why wrap it in a stasis field like this, for anyone to find? Yes, they were out in the bands and far from Currents, but the presence of the asteroid mine still made it a fairly well-traveled route.

"Hard to say," Pitorski said. "We need the logs."

Gareth ran his finger along the twisted metal until he met the resistance of the field, but he didn't push his jaevin-coated fingers any further. Merely felt at the place where the stasis field had replaced the seam of the hull. He found himself wondering if they could pump life support into this pocket. Would the stasis field contain the atmosphere? Or would it leak out? The ship certainly didn't have gravity boosted; they were using their mag boots to clomp through the ripped-up corridor.

"There's a strong reading there," Escher said. "Move your sensors closer to that spot, Commander. It's like... it's reading like a plasma charge. Only different."

"Different," Sands repeated. "That's so specific."

"Scientists don't guess, ensign," Escher snapped. "It's like, but it's different, and that's what I know until I test it."

To Gareth's surprise, Sands actually muttered an apology.

"It's present throughout the field," Escher added. "It's just stronger in some places."

"Could it have come from inside the hauler?" Pitorski was studying the opposite edge of the hole, with Sands still crouched in the middle while the rest of the team watched the corridors.

"Looks that way," Gareth said. "Let's find the bridge."

They knew for a fact that the CTF had attacked this vessel. Striker and his buddies had done so using Fleet corvettes, either stolen or manufactured with plans that Gareth's traitorous intelligence director had passed on. The corvettes had then moved on to the HTR-79 asteroid mine; the few survivors had attested to their presence.

But it wouldn't do them any good to jump to conclusions.

Using the typical hauler schematics they'd downloaded into their helmets, Pitorski led the way up to the bridge. Past more blown-out sections of hull and, in a couple of places, through pockets of stasis field that had closed around detached sections of the ship. It was slow going, and Gareth had to work to maintain his focus, zeroing in on the rhythmic sound of his breathing in his helmet as he reminded himself to watch his step, to notice his surroundings. Too easy to let panic reign in a place like this.

He had doubts as to whether they'd find anything intact on the bridge, anything worth sifting through at all. Or any recognizable bridge. It could be blown halfway to Torrent by now. But this was the job. If they found nothing, they'd pursue a Plan B. That was the way of things.

In the end, though, the stasis field had done its job. Gareth couldn't say *why* an attacker would want to preserve such a crime scene; perhaps they'd never expected it to be found. But after a tricky passage up a half-frozen ladder, they emerged into what was unmistakably the ship's control center. The ladder spilled them out onto a raised platform in the center of a tight circle. Clearly designed to let the shift commander see everything on the ring of consoles with a quick step in one direction or another. Not a bad setup, especially for a ship that should never have to see a battle.

But these long-haul voyages between the Systems encountered plenty of dangers that would necessitate quick thinking and seamless commands. Lone asteroids, pockets of debris. Pirates, absolutely, though the Fleet tried to keep those at bay.

Here, for the first time, there were bodies. Gareth didn't want to see them, but he couldn't bring himself to look away, either. A few of them were strapped into their chairs, heads bent at strange angles, limbs frozen stiff. Others had been on their feet when the blow fell, and the sudden loss of gravity had divided them from the floor, leaving them to float until they reached the ceiling. None of them were wearing suits. More evidence that they'd been caught unawares.

These were the people who kept the galaxy running, hauling supplies to distant mines. They should have been protected.

Gareth forced himself to focus on the task at hand. He mourned these people, and would continue to do so. But it would do them a disservice to let their deaths distract him.

Sands was already heading for the closest console, followed by Pitorski and one of the computer engineers who'd accompanied them in hopes of cracking some useful data out of the tech. Even exposed to the vacuum as it was, after an ambush and a too-short battle, they hoped that would be possible.

Gareth rested his wrists on the rail, watching them, until he realized he'd unintentionally taken up the commander's position. He shook his head and released the rail, then headed deliberately for the ladder. Habit. Hard to break. Yes, he still commanded the Fleet. But there was no need to cling to the role.

He ought to practice letting it go.

By the time he'd made his way down the steps to join the others, the computer engineer—a Lieutenant Waters—had coaxed the screens into displaying a turquoise line of text against the gray-black background. That looked promising.

"Any last words from the captain?" Gareth asked.

"They didn't have time." Lieutenant Waters' voice was businesslike, her eyes focused on the data. Almost convincing, but for the fact that she was a little too intent on not glancing to her left, where a dead crew person's hand still gripped the armrest. Waters plucked a data key out of her utility belt and plugged it into the console. "But the command logs were updated."

There was a grim note to her voice that he hadn't heard before. Gareth longed for the command post, suddenly, for the steadiness of the rail. "What was the last entry, Lieutenant?"

Waters straightened, the data still flowing unhindered across the screen behind her. When she met his gaze, her expression was as grim as her tone. "The captain ordered them to self destruct."

CHAPTER 4

SABRE HAD PRETTY HANGAR BAYS. Shiny floors. Lofty ceilings. And lots of space for *Moneymaker* to touch down and settle in after her little trip out to the Bone System. The flight back from Shard had been way too boring, with way too much time to think; Sloane wasn't used to leaving Current-accessible Systems for long trips out into the bands. There weren't enough entertainment modules in all the galaxy to keep her occupied, and she'd found herself pacing the length of the ship for hours at a time, trying not to think too hard about her failure to recruit the criminal bosses onto their side.

After what felt like a million years, they'd finally made it to the figurative shadow of that creepy hauler wreck, and *Sabre*'s hangar looked pretty welcoming as she stepped down *Moneymaker*'s gangplank. The band of anxiety she'd been wearing around her chest actually loosened as Gareth came striding across the hangar bay to meet the ship, her relief like a physical shedding of weight.

A feeling that immediately prompted a spike of guilt in her gut. Alex was missing, and Hilda was still unconscious in *Sabre*'s sick bay. Sloane shouldn't be feeling any kind of relief.

But Gareth was alive, and so was she. They'd made it for a few more days. If that was the fuel she needed to keep going, to keep fighting for Alex and Hilda, then she wouldn't be sorry for it.

Before she could make it to Gareth, however, Chief Escher darted past him, her flat shoes scuffling on the cement floor. Arms piled with tech. Stylus jammed behind one ear. She looked like a vid drama's interpretation of a mad scientist.

Escher swerved in front of Gareth, forcing him to slow, then barreled past Sloane, nearly knocking her aside in her rush to reach the gangplank.

"Welcome," Sloane said, twisting to watch as Escher disappeared up the gangplank. "Do come aboard?"

Gareth stopped in front of her, eyebrows raised slightly, though he wasn't looking at Escher. "She misses Alex's lab. Though I *did* tell her she needed to ask permission before moving in."

"You really ought to provide your people with better quality facilities, Fortune."

He looked tired, the skin under his eyes a bit bruised, but he smiled. Which somehow only made him look more tired, even though she knew he meant it. "You're right," he agreed. "The working conditions are truly unacceptable."

She let herself reach up to grip his arms, leaning in closer to study his face. "Have you been sleeping? I distinctly remember telling you to make sure to get enough rest, especially if you were going to go plunging into stasis fields."

His lips quirked. "I did my best to obey your orders, ma'am. Tell them to my racing thoughts next time."

That, she could understand. Before she could push to her tiptoes to kiss him, her external comm chimed with an incoming call. She took a reluctant step back, still watching him, as if part of her feared he might be a hologram.

They were all going to need *so* much therapy after this.

"Dad's calling," she said, then accepted the call, diverting it through the speaker in her fliptab so Gareth could hear. "Where are you?"

"Ready for backup in Halorin." Her father's voice came through a background of voices and footsteps, and she wondered where he was calling from. The Current, certainly—had to be, for real-time communications—but which ship had he taken? Some diplomatic vessel? One of his own?

"The crazy bots you sent me located the shield controls," Dad added. "We're ready to liberate the System, soon as you can get here."

Sloane sighed. "Do I have time for a shower at least? I smell like Shard."

"It's two days to the Current," Gareth said. "You can probably do that on the way."

Excellent. Another two days to pace and stew over her failures. "Fine. We're on our way, Dad. I'll go say goodbye to Hilda before we take off."

Chief Escher appeared back at the top of the gangplank, as if she'd been hovering back there in the shadows, waiting for Sloane to say the wrong thing. She propped her hands on her hips, scrunching her nose to adjust the position of her glasses. "Oh, no you don't. You're not taking Alex's lab. I need her equipment, and I need it here to help me figure out what this stasis field residue means."

Sloane contemplated the wisdom of propping her own hands on her hips. How far would that actually get her? "Isn't this my ship?"

BRO sniffed. Or pretended to sniff. It made a sniffing sound. "I'm my own ship, thank you very much."

Sloane didn't know whether to be impressed or concerned

that the AI was now interpreting itself as being the ship, rather than a part of it. Seemed like a bit of an identity crisis.

"Fine," Sloane said. "I guess we're taking *Sabre* to Halorin."

"Obviously," her father said, and she jumped, startled. She'd forgotten he was still on the line. "I need beetle-flipping Fleet guns, not Vin's patched together mess."

"Hey," Sloane said.

"Sorry, I mean *your* patched together mess."

Sloane shook her head, though he wasn't on holo and couldn't see her. "I meant the ship isn't a patched—you know what, never mind. Fine. *Moneymaker* stays here."

"Thank the polecats," Dad said. "See you soon."

Gareth patted her arm. "It's not a mess. It's character."

Sloane stowed her fliptab, wondering why anyone would pray to a polecat. "Right?"

It was ridiculous to have a lump in her throat because of a spaceship, and even more ridiculous to have the lump because Gareth understood how she felt. The idea of leaving *Money-maker* out here in the bands, days from the Current, while she ran off to fight a war... it made her skin itch. Yes, she'd tried hard to get rid of the ship. And she'd fallen in love with it in the process. Tale as old as time. She didn't want to leave it behind.

She didn't see that there was much of a choice. Unless she wanted to stay here in the middle of nowhere, with sparse real-time communications to tell her what was happening in Halorin. Not an option. "Brighton's in charge while I'm gone," she said. "Everyone listens to him. Even Chief Escher."

She wasn't sure Escher was still in the cargo bay, but it was worth saying, anyway.

"I want to be in charge!" BRO protested.

"Brighton's in charge," Sloane repeated.

"I need my team," Escher called, her voice echoing back from the depths of the cargo hold. Retreating to the lab, Sloane assumed, now that she'd gotten her way. At least she'd heard about Brighton, though Sloane didn't know how much good the instructions would do when she wouldn't even acknowledge orders from her Commander.

And now she wanted to bring a team. Sloane wanted to say no just out of principle.

Gareth ducked his head to peer up the gangplank. "Get them here in fifteen minutes, then. We're leaving."

Sloane looked at him, then back in Escher's direction. She wasn't sure she'd ever felt less in charge in her life. "Fine," she said again, because disagreement wasn't an option at the moment. "Bring your team. Sleep in my bed if you have to. Whatever you need."

"Sarcasm!" BRO said. "She does not want anyone in her bed!"

"Correct," Sloane muttered.

She had a feeling Gareth didn't say 'fine' nearly as often as she did. Maybe Horace Brennan had the right idea. She wasn't feeling like much of a leader at the moment. She'd only tried the clans because Candace seemed to think she had some talent for bringing disparate groups together. They had resources, after all. And no love for the CTF, despite their occasional alignment with Striker.

But they saw her as nothing more than an extension of the Fleet. And maybe they were right to.

"No one drinks my coffee," Sloane added, calling up the ramp after Escher. "No one."

There were certain fronts she'd fight to defend, leader or not.

Escher didn't reply. Sloane hoped it was because she hadn't heard, and not because she planned to find out exactly what coffee was and why Sloane was so desperate to keep it. She had half a bag left. Half of a measly bag.

She was going to cry when it ran out.

"You know," Gareth said, "you can go visit Hilda without a reason."

Reluctantly, Sloane turned her back on the ship, swallowing back a fresh wad of fear. Gareth meant to be comforting, but she'd rather have avoided the subject entirely until Hilda was up and around again. Sloane refused to acknowledge any other possibility.

She knew she could visit without a reason or an excuse. She just... wasn't all that anxious to see her friend lying in bed, asleep.

Worse than asleep. Unconscious.

When nano-healers and med cuffs and all the fancy equipment in the world couldn't snatch someone out of death's shadow quickly... well, she knew from her own studies that it was either quick or it was bad. Very bad. It was tough to face that.

But when she thought she'd be leaving, she'd figured it was better not to leave with regrets.

"Right," she said. "I'll do that. You go get some rest. You look like death."

He kissed her, lingering long enough to trace a thumb along her jaw, then stepped away with a wry smile. "Just what I love to hear."

They parted at the bay doors, Gareth headed to his cabin and Sloane splitting off toward the infirmary. Somehow, he seemed to realize that she needed to go see Hilda alone. It was hard enough to feel feelings without a witness, no matter how comfortable she was with him.

She didn't feel so comfortable on his ship. Soldiers nodded to her as she passed, some of them half raising their hands as if wondering whether they ought to salute her. Whether as their Commander's girlfriend or as a leader in her own right, she wasn't sure.

Somehow, she didn't think they'd ever saluted Gareth's ex.

Even if they did mistakenly see Sloane as a leader, she wasn't a Fleet officer. The thought was laughable. But her status was... well, if she didn't understand her role in all this, she could hardly expect the soldiers to know what to do with it. Which was why she endured a dozen such awkward encounters before she reached the doors to the sick bay.

The space was big enough to remind her that this ship was designed for battle. Rows of cots and monitors stood ready to accept a large number of casualties. The Fleet might use ships like *Sabre* to intimidate, but they were ready for the worst.

Hilda's bed was in the back corner of the space. She looked wrong in it, lying motionless as she was, both arms looped through med cuffs, her hair loosened from its braid and spread out around her head. It made her look like a beached mermaid. Somehow Sloane didn't think Hilda would appreciate that comparison. The pilot's hands looked twisted and small where they emerged from the cuffs. An IV dripped clear liquid into her veins.

Vin sat in the chair beside her bed, and though he was leaning back and reading something on his fliptab, there were dents in the covers where he'd recently been leaning on his elbows. Maybe even right up until the moment he'd heard the doors open to admit her.

Sloane stepped up to the foot of the bed, fingers twitching to pick up Hilda's chart. Instead, she closed her fingers into fists and made herself address Vin. "How is she?"

Vin snapped his fliptab shut and stowed it in his pocket. If Gareth looked tired, her uncle looked wasted. His cheekbones were pale and prominent, giving him a gaunt sort of look. His hands were trembling slightly, too, like maybe he'd gone too long without a meal.

"She's stable," he said, his voice rough with the lack of sleep. Like his grief and fear were coating his throat and wouldn't clear until Hilda was awake and yelling at him. "The doctors say there's every reason to hope she'll wake up soon. Her body's just... working to heal."

So the same, then. He was putting an optimistic spin on it, though Sloane wasn't sure if it was for her sake or for his own.

Every time she'd come to see Hilda over the last two weeks, Vin had been here. Each conversation felt like a tentative step forward, a move along the road to peace between them. He always let her make the first move. He always left it up to her. Should she suddenly retreat, or refuse to address him, she doubted he'd protest at all.

It wasn't a question of whether she wanted to make peace with her uncle. She understood, intellectually, that he was on their side now. That he was trustworthy. But she couldn't simply pretend she hadn't nearly watched him kill Gareth. She couldn't unsee the hate in his eyes.

It was going to take time.

Vin shifted in his seat, pulling himself up to stand. "I should let you have a moment with her."

Sloane held up a hand. "That's okay," she said. "I just wanted to stop by. We're heading to Halorin to help Dad free the System."

Vin glanced at Hilda, and Sloane could practically read the thoughts running through his mind. Would the ship be safe in Halorin? Or would they head into battle? Would Hilda be safer staying behind, even in *Moneymaker*'s inferior infirmary?

The same questions were running through her mind, too.

Vin sighed, then sank back into his chair. "I guess there's no safe place at the moment," he said.

True enough. Striker had seen to that.

It was quiet for a moment, and Sloane tried not to think too much about the noises of the infirmary's machines. Her time at the medical academy had rendered her immune to the instinctual fear a lot of people faced when it came to medical machinery and medicinal smells—*Sabre*'s sick bay had an undercurrent of minty menthol that grasped at her nostrils—but when it was Hilda in the bed... it just felt different, somehow.

The silence wasn't really silence. But at least it wasn't awkward, either. She focused her attention on Vin, telling herself that it wasn't because she wanted to avoid looking at Hilda. If she was going to repair her relationship with her uncle, she should probably try having a real conversation with him.

"How come you never let her know how you feel about her?" she asked.

If you were going to have a real conversation with someone, there was no use hedging. Go right for the heart, or don't bother.

She fully expected Vin to deny that there were any feelings to feel, like Hilda did. Might be tough to pull off when he hadn't left the pilot's bedside for more than fifteen minutes at a stretch since she'd been injured. But denial was easier than... feeling feelings. Sloane could relate.

Vin didn't deny it, though. He lifted a hand to press his fingertips into his forehead, looking almost pained himself. As if Hilda's injury was physically harming him, too. "You know Hilda." He tried for a smile, but it looked more like a grimace. "Sweetheart in every port."

So she claimed. Sloane had never been much for verbal filters, but in this case she really didn't want to be the one to tell him that Hilda had been pining after him for years, too. She wasn't even sure it was still true. Hilda sure claimed it wasn't.

Also, she was pretty sure the pilot would wake up just to smack her if she went around telling her secrets.

"I really should give you a moment alone," Vin said, though he didn't move to stand again. He desperately needed to get some sleep himself. Preferably in a bed, rather than dozing among the infirmary's huffing machinery.

Sloane waved the offer away. "No, no. I was just stopping by. I should go. I need to wash Shard off me, anyway."

She'd done what she could on the way out to the bands; *Moneymaker*'s showers were serviceable, but *Sabre*'s were meant for battle-crusted soldiers. Surely they'd attack the task with more gusto.

Vin cringed. He knew Shard, too. "Understood. Let me know if I can help. With Halorin."

Sloane nodded, but there wasn't a whole lot he could do. Especially not from Hilda's bedside. With a final wave, she turned for the door, doing her best not to look like she was fleeing the scene.

CHAPTER 5

THE STRANGE THING about rushing out of the bands to join a battle—or a rescue operation and potential battle, in this case—was that 'rushing' still meant two days of travel just to reach the Current and nearly another full day once they did. Which meant that Gareth had time to see to some of the administrative tasks he'd been neglecting for far too long.

As soon as *Sabre* reached the Current, Gareth had arranged a V-Space meeting with the Lostelle delegation—that was, the System leaders who were currently hiding there under Fleet protection while mounting a resistance. With significant help from his mother and Jim Lager.

Someone with clarity of forethought—maybe Lager—had rearranged the space so that it no longer resembled the theater-in-the-round that the Fleet Advisory Commission had used. Which had always felt a bit to Gareth like being at the center of an inquisition.

Instead, the space was arranged like a lounge. An almost ritzy one, maybe in Torrent or Ilya, with couches that alternated blue and gray, squat black tables complete with flickering votive candles, and no clear hierarchy to the seating arrangements.

Yes, his money was on Captain Lager. The only thing missing was an open bar.

It no longer felt like an inquisition. Though he did feel a little like a lounge singer as he stood up to address some of the most important people in the galaxy.

They hadn't sent their staff, or their representatives, as the FAC would have done. The leaders came themselves, in real time. The bulk of them were still on Lostelle: Presidents Simelda and Ash from Beck and Domer; King Lebnil of Schere; Amayra and her contingent from the Interplanetary Dwellers; Kent Wayman, who was the only free governor from Halorin; and even the Mother Balance of the isolationist Zalkalar. Gareth had thought she might leave, but the people of Zalkalar must have voted for her to stay. They made no major moves without consulting the entire population via a voting protocol.

Ilya System had also sent leaders to join them from a third location, no doubt at Zander's urging. The three of them crowded together on a single semi-circular couch, looking slightly dazed. Their planets had only been recently freed from the CTF's shield prisons, and they had the most catching up to do. But they were here, and they didn't look as if they planned to protest that. Changing times, indeed.

What hadn't changed was the fact that they were all waiting for him to speak. Even Captain Lager, who he'd asked to accompany him here. Gareth cleared his throat. He still disliked the politics part. Quite a lot.

Perhaps he ought to pretend to be a lounge singer, after all.

"We need a new structure for Fleet oversight," he said.

He probably should've welcomed them here, or put together a few words of comfort and encouragement. But even at the best of times, he preferred to get down to business. On the brink of the galaxy's destruction, he might as well take advantage of the opportunity to skip the lip service.

"That's for damn sure," King Lebnil grumbled.

A few weeks ago, the comment might have elicited nods and murmurs of agreement. Today, it caught the King a sharp elbow to the ribs from one of the Ikor System representatives. Gareth could've sworn the man had been on Lebnil's side last time.

Good. Progress.

"The Commander is the one asking for oversight." Amayra spoke in soft, musical tones that somehow still demanded attention. "Why would the Fleet ask for oversight in bad faith?"

"We've established the empire thing isn't their goal," Kent said. "Let's move on."

No one objected. Gareth glanced at Lager, who gave him a nod that felt like a thumbs-up.

"The ask is big," Gareth said. "The ask is everyone."

He paused. No one blinked out of the V-Space in outrage. No one even moved. Tough audience to read. "Specifically, the main leaders of every planet, every System, and every station in the Parse Galaxy," he continued. And this was the part they might not appreciate so much. "The ask is that the Fleet answers to the alliance, but also that the alliance answers to the Fleet."

Silence. If he'd proposed this to the FAC, even before Osmond Clay's brief takeover, there'd have been chaos.

He held up a hand as if to quiet them, even though no one had spoken. "I know the Halorin governors are unable to speak for themselves, which is a problem we plan to rectify in short order. We're on our way there now. I only ask that you consider it."

"Consider answering to the Fleet?" That was the Mother Balance, a thread of ice running through her tone. "Unprecedented."

"I disagree. We already answer to them, to an extent," President Simelda was lounging in his seat, fingers steepled across his stomach. His counterpart, President Ash, sat straight-backed in the armless chair beside his. "Under this proposal, we'd answer to each other, too."

"We govern our own people," the Mother Balance said. "We always have."

"You still would," Simelda replied. "Right, Fortune?"

Gareth hadn't expected a staunch ally from Simelda, but he appreciated the support. He nodded. "I'm merely proposing a galaxy-wide alliance. One that has us all working together, not interfering with one another. Though certainly if boundaries are crossed, or conflicts arise, we'll demand accountability." If anyone objected to that particular line item, they'd no doubt keep it to themselves. "We'll meet regularly. Share information."

If they'd shared information about the CTF early on, they might have figured out what Striker was trying to do much earlier.

"You have to understand, Fortune," one of the Ikor reps said. "Our schedules are packed tight."

Gareth blinked. He'd expected to fend off arguments about aligning with rival Systems or sharing resources. He wasn't sure he had an answer for 'I'm too booked to worry about the fate of the galaxy.'

"Your schedules," Kent Wayman repeated. Hard to ignore the disgust in his tone. "That's your issue with an alliance? That once every six months you'd have to attend a meeting?"

In Ikor's defense, it would probably be a long meeting.

The rep flushed. "I'm just saying—"

"No one cares," Simelda drawled.

"Actually," Gareth said, "I do care. And I'd like to give you an opportunity to discuss this without my presence."

That surprised them. Glances were exchanged. Shifting was done, though the V-Space eliminated any scraping of chairs—couches, in this case—or rustling of clothes. But Gareth meant what he said. An actual alliance, and the Fleet a part of it. Not off to the side, but intricately connected. If he couldn't trust the Systems to discuss it alone, then he couldn't trust them as part of an alliance. Simple as that.

And he needed to leave the Fleet with an alliance he trusted. He had to.

"One question." Simelda sat up on his couch, pressing a thumb to his bottom lip as if whatever he wanted to say was sure to come with a bad taste, and he wanted to brace himself for it. "What about Alisa March?"

A bad taste, indeed. Alisa March believed Gareth was a traitor who'd murdered the entire Fleet Advisory Commission. Alisa March was one of the only leaders in the galaxy—perhaps *the* only leader, but a powerful one—who remained on Striker's side in this fight.

Alisa March had been like an aunt to him all his life. The months that'd passed hadn't dulled the wound her lack of faith had inflicted. A childish part of him wanted to cut her out of the plan entirely. Or maybe it was a self-preserving piece; hard to say.

But the three planets she controlled ought to have a chance for representation with the alliance. They had to try.

"See if you can talk to her," Gareth said. Sour words. Very. "Maybe she wants out of her CTF alliance. She's certainly more likely to speak to you than to me."

Maybe she'd see reason. If not, at least they could say they'd tried. When they won this conflict—they *had* to win it—then perhaps they could bring her before the alliance to answer for her choices. And ensure that her planets were represented, one way or another.

Simelda nodded. When no one else moved to ask another question, Gareth said, "I'll leave you to it. Captain?"

Lager nodded, and they exited the meeting together. Trust. He *had* to trust them.

Gareth blinked away the momentary disorientation that came with dropping out of the V-Space and back into the strat room on *Sabre*'s bridge. Lager was sitting upright in his chair, somehow managing to look both engaged and relaxed at the same time. Gareth should ask for lessons in that.

"You think Alisa will talk to them?" Lager asked. "Really?"

Gareth shrugged. Alisa's trio of planets had a long history of enmity with Beck and Domer, but those two planets were under different leadership now. "We have to at least try to get everyone. If I'm going to pass command to you, we need a legitimate way to do it."

A reason he hadn't mentioned in the full meeting. He'd considered it, but the fate of the Fleet's leadership wasn't the most convincing reason for the System leaders to form an alliance. His most compelling personal reason, maybe, but not the most compelling for all.

Lager leaned his elbows on the table, clasping his hands. "Why are you acting like you don't expect to survive this?"

It was the question of a friend, not a subordinate officer. Gareth studied his friend, wondering if it would be prudent to mention the way the Current's song was battering at his brain, the almost-pain that he carried constantly whenever he traveled in it now. There was no guarantee that Escher would figure out what was going on, or that the residue in that stasis field would yield any actionable way to stop what was beginning to feel like an ongoing illness.

In a deep and abiding way, Gareth didn't expect to survive this. And even if he did, he planned to leave the Fleet.

But he'd be damned if he left it to fall apart without him.

"We just need something in place," he said finally.

"Oh, sure," Lager said, "because that long pause doesn't make me think you're lying. Not at all."

"It's not a lie," Gareth protested. "It's an evasion. Because I don't have an answer for you."

Lager just shook his head, but when Gareth stood, he didn't press the matter. Gareth clapped him on the shoulder as they headed for the door, hoping it would pass for an apology, at least for the moment. "Come on, Captain," he said. "We'll be in Halorin soon."

CHAPTER 6

THE SHIP DAD had brought into battle was an interstellar cruiser, the Ilyan make clear in the long, lean design and the artfully scalloped edges on the portholes. It'd been modified to accommodate faster engines, state-of-the-art shield technology, plasma cannons, and even a rail gun, but there was no hiding the fact that it'd obviously been built to serve as a limo, or maybe a cruiseliner. Certainly not a battleship.

Sloane was jealous of that rail gun. Gareth claimed *Money-maker* would tip over if she tried to add one to it, but she kept thinking it might be worth a shot. If you tipped over in space, up and down would just switch places. No big deal.

As she stepped across the glassed-in bridge that connected Dad's ship to the *Sabre*, there was no denying that the vessel had been made for luxury. Starting with the picturesque name that was scrawled across the hull in a graceful metallic script: the *Starset*. Add to that the light scent of lilacs and cella blossoms in the air, the thick carpet underfoot, and the fact that everything, from the comfortable carpets to the kitschy welcome signs that pointed the way to pools and buffets, was the color of lavender... yeah. Luxury vessel for sure.

"Calming atmosphere for a warship," Gareth said, as if he could read her mind. "Is that a bubble machine?"

Sloane followed his gaze to where a small tube was spitting lavender-tinted bubbles out of the ceiling. "Yes. Yes, it is."

One of the bots they'd lent to her father came whirring down the hall, moving more slowly on the carpet than it had in *Money-maker*'s metal-plated halls. Which were much more normal, unless you wanted microfibers and caught-up dust kicking around the inner workings of your ship whenever you lost gravity.

Yes, she cared about those sorts of things these days. It was no longer much of a surprise.

The bot was vaguely shaped like a cone, and it had what looked like a brass plate screwed to its head like appendage. "Oops," it said. "Forgot to turn that one off."

It unfolded a long claw toward the ceiling and slipped a tile aside. The bubbles stopped. "Such a shame," the bot said. "The effervescence has ended. Another corner of joy snuffed out by darker forces. Will we be next?"

Sloane was used to the bots' quirky personalities. Still, that was a new one. "What's with the bot?" she asked.

Her father joined them from the end of the hall, stepping forward with businesslike intention to wrap her in a brief hug. Which was very un-Zander-like. If Dad was going to be a hugger now, she'd need to adjust her views on the world. "I was hoping you could tell me," he said. "It wants a chicken-chipping pencil and paper. What does a bot need pencil and paper for?"

The bot turned a sad circle in the center of the hall. Sloane read the motion as a sigh, or maybe a shrug. If not some kind of strange funeral dance. "Artistic integrity."

Sloane looked at Gareth. He'd spent the most time with the bots on *Moneymaker*. But he just shrugged. "The copper bot is a poet."

"Copper bot," the bot repeated. "I like that. Could mean a coin, or a representative of the long arm of the law. You may call me that."

Gareth grimaced, like he wasn't sure what he'd have done if the bot had objected to the name.

Dad sighed. "I'd ask if the bots are necessary, but they hunted down Halorin's shield controls, and they did it fast. Striker's hiding them on Ve Station."

That made sense. Striker had taken Ve early on, and keeping the tech there meant he could shield all the full-on planets in the System. So far, he'd never kept the controls on a shielded planet itself, which the Fleet scientists interpreted to mean that it likely couldn't be done.

Of course, the man did love his symbols, his little inside jokes with himself. No doubt Ve meant something to him. Symbol of the galaxy's selfishness, maybe. She could see him lacking the self-awareness to catch the irony in that.

Or maybe he just hated some actor who kept a home there. Hard to know.

Dad gestured for them to follow him down the hall, in the direction that, according to the kitschy lavender sign, would lead them to the gravity playground and performance-art extravaganza. Whatever that meant.

"I'm going to assume the bridge is this way, too," Sloane said as he led the way down the corridor.

"You mean the Captain's Party Plaza?" Gareth asked, pointing to the sign.

"The whimsy is juxtaposed with our warlike situation," the copper bot said.

Sloane couldn't disagree. Especially when they reached the bridge to find that when the *Starset* signs promised a party, they followed through.

Instead of a command center, the bridge featured a circle of couches, not unlike the ones she'd seen on smaller atmo cruisers. Though she'd never seen one with a disco ball before. It was hard not to feel as if the captain was meant to lounge here while half-interested sailors worked the controls that ran around the circumference of the room. Probably while wearing lavender-colored hats.

Personally, she wasn't sure how safe she'd feel on an interstellar cruise where the motto above the door read 'If you need me, I'll be dancing.'

She could only hope it was all for show. A little atmosphere for when they gave tours to the VIPs, or something.

She'd barely taken in the rhinestone-crusted designs on the backs of the console chairs before her mother leapt out of one of them, rushing across the room to crush her into a tight hug. Sloane hadn't seen her mother since Mom had woken her in the night to warn her to get off Elter in a hurry. She hugged her back.

"Lissie?" she asked.

Mom stepped back with clear reluctance, wiping her cheek quickly. "Over there."

Her sister was sitting beside an older man whose monitors showed maps and navigation to one side, ship stats on the other. Sloane would have bet anything the man was piloting this showboat; Lissie had made no secret of her piloting aspirations. Her brow was knit in concentration as she peered over the pilot's shoulder, watching the screen. He wasn't instructing her, but he didn't look annoyed by her presence, either.

Lissie had inherited their mother's blonde features, where Sloane matched her father's dark-haired looks. Lissie's was the kind of blonde that was hard to pin down, tinting toward brown instead of platinum or golden, though she'd been white-blonde as a baby. She had their mom's heart-shaped face, too, and more delicate features than Sloane's, though her legs stretched long beside the console. She might have passed Mom in height by now.

She looked so much older than she had even a few months ago on Elter. How old *was* she now? Sixteen? Seventeen? That couldn't be right.

Sloane went over to her sister, giving her a tap on the shoulder. "Hey, Lissie," she said. "Giving them hell as usual?"

Lissie glanced up at her. Or rolled her eyes. It was hard to tell when she flicked them back to the screens so quickly. "No one calls me that anymore. I go by Felicity."

Sloane blinked, surprised by the vitriol in her sister's tone. And, even more, by the unspoken addendum that Lissie left out, but was nonetheless loud and clear, anyway: 'Not that you would know.'

Could Sloane blame her? She couldn't even remember her sister's *age*. Had she even spoken to her sister when she and the crew had passed through Elter a few months back? She couldn't recall. She didn't think she had.

But she remembered the important things, didn't she? Like Lissie's aspirations to become a pilot. She remembered that.

Except that it was *Felicity*, not Lissie. That would take some getting used to.

Sloane backed away, keeping a careful smile on her face even though it felt like a lie. "Sorry," she said. "Felicity."

She waited a beat, though she wasn't exactly sure what she was waiting for. The name to serve as a password, maybe. As if using it would prompt her sister to get up and hug her.

Didn't happen. Hardly a surprise.

When Sloane turned away to join the others, Mom was there with an apologetic look on her face. "She's been through a lot," she said softly. "It's been hard."

Yeah. Locked on her own planet for weeks. Grounded, without even a view of the stars to comfort her, and wondering if she'd live to see the next morning—and if she did, whether that would be a good thing. Or if she'd have to endure a slow expiration while the crops failed and the planet cooled or warmed to unendurable temperatures.

All while her sister had been gallivanting around the galaxy. Saving other people before bothering with Lissie.

But Sloane *had* saved them. "It's totally understandable," she said, and even though her Mom's anxiety melted into a smile—a genuine one, not like Sloane's forced facade—the lump in her throat didn't dissolve. If anything, it just got thicker.

There were consequences to abandoning your family to go hopping from planet to planet like an overly bouncy zeeball. She'd known that. She just hadn't expected them to be quite so... personal. But that was her fault, not Lissie's. Felicity's.

Gareth was already seated on one of the couches across from her father, looking decidedly uncomfortable amid all the cushions. Sloane set her sister's anger aside for the moment and went to join him, settling in by the arm of the sofa. Where an enticing array of buttons invited her to order a beverage.

Well. While on a cruise ship. Sloane punched in an order, and within thirty seconds the chair had presented her with a tall glass filled with a tropical yellow drink. Laced through with enticing threads of red, it was capped with a beach umbrella. Pineapple and pomegranate.

When she looked up, everyone was staring at her.

"What?" she said. "It's non-alcoholic. I don't drink and mission."

Gareth laughed. The rest of them—her parents, the captain, and even the copper bot—just continued to stare at her. For so long that she thought the universe might have glitched and frozen them in place until she caught Felicity shaking her head out of the corner of her eye.

"I miss Damian," she muttered. Gareth patted her hand.

"If everyone has what they need," her father said, pointedly raising his eyebrows at her drink, "I'll go over the mission specs."

He didn't wait for her response, which made that a rhetorical statement. Cushy as this place was, the central console did feature a holo projector. Meant for entertainment, she assumed, but Dad used it to pull up a model of a station she'd never seen before. It was shaped like an hourglass, the top bulging slightly thicker than the bottom. The middle looked ragged, like it'd been shaped with an axe. Maybe it had detachable sections?

"Striker blew out Ve Station's central docks to prevent anyone from escaping," Dad said. "The private berths are also inaccessible."

For a second, she didn't understand what he was saying. The words didn't match the model in front of them.

Except that they *did*. Sloane felt her entire face go numb as understanding hit her like a two-ton cargo crate. *"That's* Ve Station?"

Her voice came out as a horrified whisper. If that was Ve Station, Striker had hacked the place to bits.

The guy was more impulsive than she gave him credit for. And more destructive. She tried not to imagine how many people might have been on the docks or on ships when he'd sent his people to blow them away. Pilots, maintenance crews, security guards. Celebrities and their entourages were not the only people who made their homes on Ve Station.

Dad nodded, lips pressed into a grim line. "We'll have to approach in atmo gear. It'll be harder to see us coming that way, in any case."

Sloane took a moment to consider how unfamiliar she was with the actual specs of Dad's job. Was he some kind of strategist? She'd thought diplomat. Upscale pencil pusher, at best. Mysterious.

"Aren't they guarding the blown-out docks?" Gareth asked.

Sloane certainly would, if she'd destroyed almost a third of a station just to keep people from leaving. They already knew the rest of the station had maintained life support; the one real news piece that'd leaked out after the occupation was evidence enough. Though Sloane would have loved to know how the woman had managed that. Especially now that she could see first-hand how bad the damage was. Even without it, the scanners detected life signs within the station.

The important thing was that the integrity of the bay doors must have held, leaving only a ring of doors to guard the station from the dangers of space.

Striker already knew they wouldn't hesitate to approach in atmo gear. He'd have people waiting for them.

"They probably *are* guarding the docks," Dad agreed. "But not in large numbers. They don't *have* large numbers, which we know from our heat scans. We know approximately how many people were on the station when they invaded, so we can guess how many guards they've got."

Sure. Simple math.

"So we'll sneak in if we can, fight through if we can't," Dad continued. "Get to the shield controls, shut them off, and free Aemlyn and Camber. Plus their moons."

Sure. Nothing to it. Battle plans always sounded so easy when you were sitting on a cushy couch, sipping a tropical drink and looking at a model of a half-blown-up station.

It was never quite so easy once you actually leapt into the black.

Gareth leaned forward, placing his elbows on his knees as he studied the model. "Ve isn't a small station," he said. "Where are the shield controls located?"

"The bots isolated the signals," Dad said.

"We have many talents," the copper bot put in.

Dad jabbed a finger at the top of the model. "They're in the viewpoint park at the crown of the station, right here."

In through the doors, up through the entire top half of the station. No problem.

Sloane finished her drink and stood. "All right, let's go," she said. "Do you think we'll run into any movie stars while we're there?"

CHAPTER 7

IF SOMEONE HAD TOLD Sloane a couple of years ago that she'd be hobnobbing with Fleet soldiers, shrugging equipment on beside them and even trading a joke or two, she'd have assumed that person must've dipped their whole head in the torkfruit punch. She'd have said that the Fleet was nothing but a bunch of stuck-up, self-appointed heroes, with their heads so far up each other's space suits that they had no idea what actual heroism looked like.

And now she was prepping for a mission with them. Again.

Gareth was securing his atmo gear, flicking zippers and buttons with practiced ease while simultaneously watching his soldiers. Like he wanted to check their work, or jump in if anyone needed help.

He caught her watching him, and his fingers paused on the fasteners. "Do I have something on my face?"

Sloane returned to her own gear with a shrug. "Remember that time we only had one rocket? Good times. Until we got to the surface and you were framed for murder."

She was well aware that she was somewhere between rambling and worrying—not that those two things were mutually exclusive—but somehow, she couldn't keep herself from talking, anyway. That fritzy filter again.

"We *had* more rockets," he said. "You just weren't qualified to operate one."

"And I am now?"

"No, I just got tired of arguing with you about it."

"Also, you're sleeping with me."

"Also that." He could pretend he wasn't embarrassed, but the reddening tips of his ears made that a complete lie. "Why the nostalgia, all of a sudden?"

She shrugged, fussing with the hem of her suit. "Just feeling antsy."

He stepped closer, reaching up to adjust the tie at the collar of her suit. "We'll have a platoon with us this time. No going it alone."

As if summoned by that promise, Captain Pitorski strode over, her own helmet already in place. "Ready to get going, sir?"

Gareth nodded, stepping back so he could secure his helmet over his head.

"Does she ever sleep?" Sloane asked, following suit. "I feel like she's with you on every single mission."

He glanced at Pitorski, considering. "I think she reprogrammed her genes to eliminate the need."

"Ha, ha," Pitorski said. "Get moving, sir, before I kick you off the mission."

He schooled his expression to one of solemn obedience. "Understood, Captain."

Even though he commanded the entire Fleet and therefore outranked Pitorski, she was in charge of ground missions. Or in this case, station missions. He claimed he'd once had trouble stepping back, but Sloane saw no evidence of that now.

With everyone suited up, the doors trundled open, and the team leapt into the black. Ve Station sparkled ahead, beautiful despite of its ruptures. She'd always wanted to visit here, but even with Dad's connections, that wasn't an easy card to draw. Vin had managed it once, a long time ago.

She hadn't quite pictured visiting like this. Though it *was* pretty fun to operate her own rocket. Circumstances being what they were, she'd agreed to follow the instructions to the letter.

Next time they rocketed without Pitorski staring them down, she'd coax Gareth into racing with her. She'd definitely win.

A station like Ve was never going to have the kind of beehive-like traffic that a lot of stations boasted. This was a VIP station, a crème de la crème situation. The people who lived here were award-winning actors and musicians, household names, and the place was made for that. Lux to the max. No one else could afford to buy a churro from a cart in the park, let alone an apartment. The population was small, the visitor list exclusive. Not many ships coming and going, or so she imagined.

Even so, the absolute stillness was unnerving. Every station she'd ever seen had at least a couple of ships hanging around for security. Sometimes drones, sometimes human operated. But always present.

Here, everything stood motionless, like the entire station had been wrapped in its own stasis field.

Which was why she noticed the ripple.

It wouldn't have been visible otherwise. And it wouldn't have been noticeable if she hadn't been staring at the station as she moved toward it, imagining all the high-powered hostages that must be pacing the lengths of their rooms like fairy-tale royalty trapped in a cluster of towers.

One minute, she was thinking of fairy tales. The next, a ripple. It was like someone had dropped a coin gently into a pool, disturbing the images reflected on the surface of the water without destroying them entirely. The ripple reverberated, sending gentle blips skittering around the image of the station.

Like someone was up there flopping a big, Ve-Station-colored cloth.

A blink, then two, and the ripples stopped.

"Did you see that?" Sloane asked through the comms.

"See what?" Pitorski replied.

She'd take that as a 'no.' "Something's wrong," Sloane said. "Are we sure the station is even there?"

That'd be a new level of intrigue, faking an entire station. A hologram or something? Striker did have a good chunk of the Interplanetary Dwellers' stash of alien tech. Who knew what he could do with it?

"We're detecting its power signatures," Gareth said. "Heat, light. Movement."

Okay, maybe so. But that didn't explain the ripples. "Something's wrong," she insisted.

"There's nothing on the scanners," Pitorski said.

"Well, your scanners suck. Use your eyes. Look, it's happening again."

Pitorski held up a hand, instructing the team to pause. They floated, occasionally firing their rockets to keep their bodies floating upright in relation to the station.

If only past Sloane could see herself now. Ordering Fleet soldiers around. Well, it wasn't the ordering part that would have surprised her so much as the fact that they were following those orders.

Come to think of it, past Pitorski would probably be equally shocked by this turn of events.

She waited. And the station *shimmered*. It really did look like someone was shaking a cloth. Weird as hell.

"I'll be damned," Pitorski breathed.

"I'm right from time to time," Sloane said. "What *is* that?"

Pitorski didn't respond. But Gareth said, "Striker's got ships there."

Sloane twisted to look at him, which sent her spinning in a full circle before she could right herself. "I don't see any ships."

He extended an arm toward the station. "They're stealthed. It's Fleet tech. Stealth works fine in open space, even in atmo. It's easy to grab the reflections around you when it's a blanket of stars or sky, clouds, what have you. But against something like a station..."

"Too many details," Sloane said. "The tech gets glitchy."

"Exactly," he replied.

So much for Dad's pretty hologram battle plan. "So it's guarded."

"We knew there could be a fight." That was Sands, speaking up from wherever he was floating out there among the platoon. Hard to make out individuals when they all looked like specks of dust in suits. Big specks of dust, but still. "I say we go in."

"Not your call, Ensign," Pitorski said.

"He's got a point, though," Gareth said. "We expected guards."

Sure. Otherwise, why bring soldiers at all? Sloane glanced at Pitorski, the closest among the specks. Aside from Gareth. She couldn't see the Captain's face, but the woman had to be doing the same mental calculations that were running through Sloane's head right now.

"We planned to fight guards," Sloane said. "Not *ships*. We'll never get up to the park this way. We need another way in."

Gareth groaned. "Please don't say the garbage."

"I doubt Ve Station *collects* garbage like your people do, Fortune." Her brain was clicking, reaching for puzzle pieces. Reaching for a plan. "No garbage. But the park has a window ceiling. It's a viewpoint."

"We can't cut through it," Gareth said, already following her logic. "It'll decompress."

Sloane scanned the station, letting her gaze linger on the

clear dome that capped the top of the thing. The shield controls were all the way up there. Why go the long way when you could cut a path straight to what you wanted? That was one of the many benefits of space travel.

Another thought to which she'd have objected heavily a few years ago. How times changed.

"Decompression's the idea," she said.

Before she could lay out the new plan, another ripple shuddered through the station. And this time, it kept right on rippling, until it felt like the whole station would be torn apart by the waves. She didn't have time to ask what that was about before the stealth barrier dropped away, revealing a ship that was shaped like an arrowhead, with mean looking cannons dotted along the edges.

It was one of Striker's stolen Fleet corvettes. And it was coming straight for them.

CHAPTER 8

GARETH ALWAYS THOUGHT it would be nice if, just once, a plan they made would survive first contact with the enemy.

But that'd never been the case in any operation he'd ever undertaken. And it certainly wasn't the case now, as the enemy corvette flickered into sight just to twitch away from the station and head straight in their direction.

So much for catching them by surprise.

"Are they listening in on our comms?" Pitorski asked.

Sloane grabbed for Gareth's arm, missed, and grabbed a second time, this time managing to look her arm around his elbow. "One way to find out. We'll proceed on the altered mission. You hold them off."

"Hold off a corvette," Pitorski said. "They'll barbecue us in five seconds."

The corvette's cannons flared, as if responding to a challenge.

"Get back to *Sabre*," Gareth said. "Captain Lager, cover the platoon's retreat. Hopefully that'll be distraction enough. Zander, ask the copper bot to scan for life signs in the park. I won't risk accidentally spacing civilians."

If Pitorski objected to his jumping in with orders, she didn't show it.

"Covering, sir," Lager said.

"In search of the lonely stargazer," the copper bot said.

Zander just cursed. Something about the progeny of a zebra combined with a giraffe. Gareth decided to take it as an agreement.

"What if they *are* listening to our comms?" Sloane hissed.

There wasn't anything to be done about it. "Then we'd better hurry."

A streak of plasma arced across the black above them, a blinding flash that seared across the backdrop of darkness as *Sabre* fired on the corvette. He could almost imagine the heat scorching the outside of his suit, though he didn't truly feel any change in temperature. There was nothing to carry the heat out here, even without the environmental controls in his suit.

Still, it felt much too close.

Gareth engaged his rocket, spiraling away from the fight and directing them toward the foot of Ve Station. They'd have to loop around to skim up the other side and hope no other stealthed ships caught sight of them.

"Shouldn't we make sure the platoon makes it to *Sabre*?" Sloane asked.

Every cell in his body wanted to do just that. But his training had taught him otherwise; he had to follow his own orders first. "We trust them to do their jobs, they trust us to do ours. Come on."

His sensors warned him of the battle flashing behind them, but he kept his focus ahead. They rocketed toward the station, and he hoped every eye would be trained on the battle behind them, that no one would notice two specks inching their way out of the station's damaged beltway. The station was still rippling around the middle, indicating that more ships were indeed stealthed and waiting. But no one broke off to fire at them.

Yet. It was always yet. Didn't matter; not when there was no contingency plan. The one option left on the table was 'keep going.'

Once they cleared the ragged middle section of the station, Ve's outer hull smoothed out into the expected network of ladders and walkways. Which Gareth and Sloane ignored, using their rockets instead, but it was comforting to see that the rest of the station's infrastructure remained intact.

They'd made it halfway up the outside of the station when his comm chimed. "No life signs in the park," the copper bot reported.

To Gareth's surprise, the bot didn't add any flowery commentary to its announcement. Maybe Zander was getting through to it.

Or maybe safety and evacuation were too boring to inspire poetics.

Behind them, *Sabre* pulsed reddish-orange streams of energy at the corvette, which was using its smaller size to dodge the blows and return fire. The shots fizzled harmlessly into *Sabre*'s shields, for now. Gareth couldn't tell from here whether Pitorski and the others had managed to make it to the frigate. He'd have to assume that they had.

It felt like an age before he and Sloane reached the bubble-like protrusion at the top of Ve Station. When they did, Gareth eased himself down on the clear window to peer inside.

"Do you have explosives in that suit?" Sloane asked. "Or a really big axe?"

Gareth squinted, trying to see through the double panes of his visor and the station's viewing dome. "No. I simply want visual confirmation that there are no civilians there."

All he could see was a mess of reflections. The only hint of what lay beyond the viewport was a greenish tint to the window, suggesting vegetation. But only because that was what he'd expect to see there; it might just as well have been a swimming pool, or a vat of gelatin.

"I can't see anything but wavery green light," Sloane said.

Still, he let his scanners run a final check. The bot's would be more accurate, but he had to double check.

Sloane rapped on the window with her suited fist. "So, how do we blow this thing?"

Gareth stared at her. "You don't have a plan for that?"

She frowned into the window, like it might give her an answer. "Why would *I* have a plan for that? You're the soldier who knows things about materials and explosions."

"Maybe because it was your plan in the first place?"

She shook her head. Like he'd suggested Ve Station might be made of cheese and that they ought to try and chew their way in. "Honestly, Fortune, sometimes I don't know what to do with you. Hey, Lager, have you got an extra cube ship lying around?"

A beat. "Define 'extra,'" Lager said.

"One you won't need again."

"Oh, well, in that case, yes."

Gareth shook his head. "We could have just sent it over here in the first place."

Sloane lifted a finger. "Someone needs to recover the shield controls."

"Zander," Gareth said, "would you send a bot to retrieve the shield controls when the park depressurizes?"

"Showoff," Sloane grumbled.

Sometimes, the most obvious answer was the best one.

"The copper guy can go," Zander said. "It's not doing anything."

A sound of protest, halfway between a gasp and a gurgle.

And then the copper bot said, "I am of a delicate constitution and wont to lose consciousness before my task has been completed."

Gareth wasn't sure anyone had ever sounded so indignant before, in the entire history of people—and bots—being asked to complete distasteful tasks. He wasn't sure what the bot found distasteful about retrieving boxes of tech from blown-out parks, but the copper bot's tone made it very clear how it viewed the assignment.

"Rather send you than one of the quiet ones," Zander complained.

"I shall chain myself to the pilot's seat in protest. I shall sing songs of woe until my voice chip wears out. I shall—"

"*These* are the bots you found?" Zander asked.

Sloane shrugged, and Gareth could see her grinning behind her visor. "I like him."

"I'll send the big round guy over," Zander said. "He's jovial enough."

Gareth hadn't seen that one, but as long as it didn't protest its job description, it would work just fine.

Sloane pushed back from the window, then ignited her rocket. "Best clear out."

They had a front-row view of the cube ship as it left *Sabre*'s bay. Three cube ships, actually, and Gareth recognized the wisdom in it as they feigned a rear attack on the corvette, covering the purpose of the third ship and demanding the corvette's attention as it sneaked away from the battle and zoomed straight for Ve Station. Lager was, as always, an excellent strategist.

Gareth couldn't see Zander's round bot leaving the *Starset*—he could barely make out the cube ships, in truth—but he assumed it was on its way, too.

And then the cube ship slammed into Ve Station's park. The dome shattered, the air venting suddenly and dramatically as Ve spewed a stream of glass, trees, and colorful vendor carts into the vacuum. He recognized the distinctive lacework of a famed Ve Station bridge railing.

"Wagner Penn is going to be so pissed," Gareth said, picturing how red the Ve Station's governor's face would be the next time they met.

"Station already needs repairs." Sloane was backing toward *Sabre*, her rockets firing gently as she took in the scene. She looked like she was doing a back float through a universe-sized swimming pool. "What's a few more?"

Those trees were probably worth several million on their own. The bridges? He didn't want to think about the bridges.

"Going in," an unfamiliar bot's voice said. "Isolating shield controls for destruction."

"Farewell, sweet friend," the copper bot said.

"It's actually quite pleasant out here," the new bot said. "In addition to the shield control boxes, I see a statue of a dog. And the wheel of a cart. And a frozen churro."

"I shall sing of your deeds until—"

"Planetary shields are coming down," Zander interrupted.

There was cheering in the background, as well there should be. Even the copper bot said, "Freedom never tasted so sweet as when it was denied."

"Little good you did," Zander replied.

"I'm sending a cube ship to pick you up," Lager said. "Hold tight."

Gareth turned to Sloane, expecting her expression to be a bright one. They'd released Halorin System from the CTF's shields, saving millions of lives. And with the governors freed, their list of allies would grow—no matter how angry Wagner Penn might act.

Striker wouldn't be able to hold out much longer.

But Sloane wasn't smiling. She was staring past Ve Station, her attention locked on Aemlyn in the distance. Her lips were parted in shock, and she kept blinking, like she couldn't quite understand what she was seeing.

Gareth fired his rockets gently, swiveling around so he could follow her gaze to where a huge shimmering line burned across the space between Aemlyn and Ve. He squeezed his eyes shut, then opened them again, trying to understand what it was he was seeing. A weapon? A beam of energy? A... could it be a ship?

"How did he get Alex to *do* it?" Sloane breathed. "She would never. She couldn't."

Gareth's stomach went cold. "Don't tell me."

"It's a wormhole," she said.

He stared at it. From this angle, it looked like a shimmering pool of mercury. He couldn't see what lay beyond it. After a moment, though, it became clear that the pool was growing wider by the second.

Not for the first time, Gareth wished he'd asked Sloane about her adventures in that other galaxy. And about what methods she'd used to get there.

"We've got a worse problem," Lager said.

Gareth wasn't sure he'd ever heard a more ominous statement in his life. He forced himself to turn his back to the wormhole, so he was once again facing Sloane and *Sabre*. Whatever Lager was about to say, Gareth had a feeling he and Sloane had better get back to the ship. And soon.

"Worse than a universe-destroying wormhole opening up above one of the most populous planets in the galaxy?" Sloane asked.

If it really was capable of destroying the universe, Gareth doubted it mattered where the thing appeared. But he agreed with the central point.

"Could be," Lager said. "There are ships leaving the planets. And they're coming in enormous numbers."

Gareth shook his head, not understanding. "Isn't that a good thing?"

"Their weapons are hot," Lager replied.

Sloane squeezed her eyes shut, then opened them, like she wanted to pinch herself and make it all disappear. "Let me guess. You're not going to say they're aiming at Striker, are you?"

"Unfortunately, no," Lager replied. "They're aiming straight at us."

CHAPTER 9

SLOANE DIDN'T LOVE RULES. In her mind, even the most rigid of them were pretty much just suggestions. Often, it was hard not to view them as straight-up challenges.

She couldn't help it. That was just how she was built.

Yet even she understood that Alex's no-wormhole rule was a non-negotiable one. Okay, except for two *tiny* little exceptions. But they'd been important ones. And since then, she'd decided to view the universe as a wormhole-free place. Alex knew her stuff; she wouldn't have sacrificed her life's work for a 'maybe this will be a problem.' Without a way to stabilize the wormholes, they could *de*stabilize the universe. End of story.

When the universe made a rule, Sloane figured it'd probably be best to listen.

Striker, on the other hand, didn't appear to see the potential destruction of the entire universe as a deal-breaker.

As she and Gareth retreated back to *Sabre*, pushing their rockets as hard and fast as possible, Sloane couldn't help but stare at the expanding pool of the wormhole. She'd never seen one out against the vacuum like this, and she'd never seen one so large. She kept trying to convince herself that she was imagining things.

That someone had unfolded a shiny circus tent out in the middle of space, or spilled a vat of mercury that'd somehow managed to shape itself into a flat puddle. Despite the lack of gravity, or air, or anything.

If it turned out to be an illusion, she wouldn't even feel silly. She'd just be relieved.

But by the time she and Gareth made it to *Sabre*'s bridge, the wormhole had expanded to the frigate's size. Maybe even larger. It was hard to tell, exactly. Yet it was all too clear that the broad side of the wormhole was aimed straight at Aemlyn. Ve Station orbited the planet at a distance, like a teenager pretending not to follow their parent through a mall, but the planet's signature pinkish-orange sands were unmistakable.

As was the group of ships that spun away from the planet like a volley of shooting stars. She wouldn't have been able to see them without the magnification on *Sabre*'s viewport, so it was one hundred percent imagination that convinced her she could make out their cannons from here.

Even *Sabre* couldn't stand up to that bunch of ships *and* what was left of the CTF's fleet at Ve Station. She swallowed hard when she caught a quick view of the *Starset* bobbing nearby. Dad's ship might've been outfitted with weapons, but it was still just a cruiseliner. Those ships would crush it in minutes.

"Better take a look at this, sir," one of the officers said. "Splitting screen to show a Current view."

Sloane expected Gareth to step forward, but it was Lager who made a sound of agreement. This was his ship now, his captaincy. Pitorski and Sands were standing next to him on Sabre's little balcony area—it probably wasn't called that, but that was what it looked like—and unlike Gareth and herself, they'd had time to shed their atmo gear for blue on-ship fatigues.

When the viewport split, Sloane gasped.

She'd seen the Current's colors shift before, so though it was alarming to see the blue-green flow dulled to a smoky gray, it wasn't all that new. But she hadn't seen the Current sparkling with flashes of yellow lightning, jagged tears that ripped through the darkness like a storm.

"He's doing it," she said. "He's imploding the universe."

And the Current was flashing warnings like a frantic traffic light.

What the hell had Striker done to get Alex to agree to this? She knew the risks better than anyone.

"Some kind of feedback from the wormhole, maybe," Gareth said.

"Can't solve that now, sir," Lager said. "I'll hail the Aemlyn ships. They'll see reason. We did just save them."

Sloane wasn't so sure. She'd never been to Aemlyn, but she knew they had one of the stronger defense networks in the galaxy. She always thought it was a lot of nonsense, another instance of the Halorin governors acting like they ran the most important System in the galaxy.

But that might have been the Ilya-Halorin rivalry talking.

"This is the Fleet ship *Sabre,* hailing the approaching Aemlyn ships," Lager said. "Please stow your cannons. We released the shields from your planet."

Right. Maybe they thought Striker had lifted the shields so he could attack them or something. Seemed a big conclusion to jump to, but Sloane hadn't been trapped under a planet-sized cage for months on end, so she figured she didn't have room to judge.

There was no response. Lager repeated the hail as Gareth gripped the rail by his side, eyes scanning the screens ahead. He looked pale, and she had to imagine that whatever was happening to the Current was also playing out in his head.

Though honestly, she probably looked pretty pale right about now, too.

To their left, Dad's rotund ship was cruising closer to the wormhole than *Sabre*. Sloane wanted to call them back, to yell at them to get out of trouble. But she didn't need to add her voice to the hails and orders that were going on right now.

All she could really do was to watch the *Starset* and imagine what they were thinking, what they were doing. Trying to hail the Aemlyn ships too, maybe. Dad knew most of the governors by name. Maybe they'd listen to him more readily than they would a Fleet captain.

It didn't make her feel better. Her parents and sister were on that ship. She wanted to scream at them to retreat, to get out of Halorin before this went sideways.

Not that the Currents looked safe right now, either.

"Halorin can't have been colluding with the CTF," Gareth said.

"Kent would have known," Sloane said. Her voice sounded far away. "I think."

Unless he was colluding with them, too. But that was panic talking, making ridiculous suggestions in her head. If Kent had been working with Striker, he'd have betrayed the Lostelle delegation long ago.

"The Halorin planets were locked away for months," Pitorski said. "That's a big con to run."

Much as she distrusted the Halorin governors, Sloane had to agree.

Lager began hailing the ships for a third time.

Almost faster than Sloane could process it, the leading Aemlyn ship swerved, braking hard enough that she could feel sympathetic pressure in her chest from the amount of force the crew must be taking. Even with artificial gravity to help balance it out.

As soon as the ship had flipped, it fired on the vessel to its right, long red lines slicing cleanly through the vacuum. It must have hit an engine, or bypassed a shield, or something, because the second ship burst into a ball of flame, burning fast and bright as the fire consumed what oxygen it could from the ship's life support. And then it burned out, leaving a searing impression behind Sloane's eyelids.

She swallowed. "Maybe *some* of them were working for the CTF?"

"We don't have the whole story," Gareth said. "Lager, get us out of here."

"They need our help," Sands protested.

Pitorski smacked the Ensign on the back of the head. "*Sir*."

"We can't help them without backup," Gareth said.

Before Lager could give the order, a second wormhole sliced into the vacuum like a blade emerging through a vat of oil. *Two* wormholes, when for months—over a year now—Alex had refused to attempt even one more. And now there were two? Maybe Alex wasn't making them at all. Maybe Striker had tortured the secrets out of her and thrown her in a cell. Or worse.

But that had to be the panic talking. It *had* to be.

In the distance, the Current bucked and writhed like a wounded animal.

And then the Current wasn't even the secondary problem anymore as a new ship stretched out of the wormhole. Long and wide, with a ribbed exterior and a line of harsh spikes along its spine, it looked like a prehistoric fish hanging from the ceiling of a dusty museum on Darrow. Only it was big enough to fill an ocean, or at least a decent sized lake.

Those Fox Clan dragon ships were one thing. They were bizarre in their own way, but they still looked like *ships*.

She didn't know how to describe this thing without using the word 'alien.'

A pair of bulbs on the ship's spine turned, and *Sabre*'s sensors blinked red. Alien or not, the frigate recognized weapons. And it recognized when they were running hot.

One of the officers shouted a warning through the comms, but it would've been too late even if the Aemlyn vessels had been answering. The alien ship fired on the Aemlyn leader—the one that'd destroyed its brother mere minutes ago—and the Aemlyn ship vanished.

It didn't go up in a ball of flames. It didn't catch a hole in the hull and start venting atmosphere. It *dissolved*, like the molecules had been dipped in a vat of acid.

And it'd all happened in seconds.

"Battle stations," Lager said. "Prepare to fire."

Sloane wanted to grip the rail right along with Gareth, but she kept her hands at her sides. She felt more than saw the way Pitorski and Sands turn to Lager, their eyes wide. Not with concern for the battle, some part of her increasingly panicked brain informed her. No, they were surprised by Lager's order.

Sloane was all for careful steps—okay, maybe not when it came to her personal decisions, but at least she could respect them—but if there was any time to take out another vessel, it was when the thing could fire a ship-dissolving weapon. Why would Pitorski and Sands even blink an eye? Sands actually took a step toward his Captain, like he intended to protest.

She expected Gareth to step in, maybe throw them off the bridge. But when he turned to Lager, his expression mirrored their confusion. "Belay that order, Captain."

Sloane stared at him. "What?"

Another Commander might have tried to silence a civilian on the bridge, even his girlfriend. But Gareth just looked back at her, frowning, like he was trying to multiply large sums in his head. "There's no need to become the aggressors here," he said finally.

"Sir?" Lager said. "That alien ship just destroyed a Parse

Galaxy vessel. I realize they were starting their own fight, but we can't allow it to take anyone else down. Ourselves included."

Gareth just stared at him. "Alien ship," he repeated. It sounded like a question.

It sounded like he couldn't *see* it.

The other officers on the bridge were staring up at the balcony, clearly confused as to which orders they should be following. Sloane took Gareth's arm, trying to be gentle. "It's the Current," she said. "It's messing with your head. There's an alien ship out there, and it's preparing to fire. It's going to take out every ship that left Halorin."

And wipe them out of existence. The alien ship trundled toward them, its ribbed hull cracking open and expanding until it gave birth to a stream of baby alien ships, then another and another, all of them moving much too fast for anything made in the Parse Galaxy. She hadn't even seen a gap in the hull where they could have exited. It'd just expanded and expanded, and now they were here, swarming like angry wasps.

"Sir, we need to take the offensive here," Lager said. "Weapons hot, fire on my mark."

"Stand down, Captain," Gareth replied. "There are no ships out there."

But there were *dozens* of ships, zipping out of that stretchy, skin-like hull. Soon, there'd be hundreds.

Sloane was still holding on to Gareth's arm, and she squeezed it, willing him to see what she could. Willing him to see the *Starset* hovering nearby. Willing him to see how the wasp ships circled it, stingers primed, like they deemed it the main threat here. Which *was* strange, she had to admit. Why not the *Sabre*?

Her barely restrained panic felt like it was going to burst up through her throat and strangle her. If *Sabre* fired now, they might manage to avoid hitting the *Starset*, but the resulting shrapnel would be another story. She couldn't imagine that the fat cruiseliner was very dextrous. "Dad's ship is in the way," she said. "How can you fire without risking them?"

"Prepare to fire," Lager said. "If anyone gets a clear shot, take it at will."

Gareth stepped toward him. "Captain, you're out of line. I said—"

"Someone remove the Commander from the bridge," Lager interrupted.

Gareth was shaking his head in confusion as she stepped away from him, allowing two waiting soldiers to grab hold of his arms. They, at least, were ready to respond to Lager's command. A small voice in her head whispered that Pitorski and Sands had been closer, that she'd have expected them to be the ones to take him. Why hadn't they moved?

It didn't matter. Not when the alien ships had nearly obscured her father's cruiser. She imagined Lissie—Felicity— with her view to the stars once again obscured.

She didn't even see the alien ships fire. One moment she was looking at the cruiseliner, imagining her sister craning her neck to try and see around the surrounding alien fighters. And the next, she was watching as her father's ship turned to mist.

CHAPTER 10

GARETH LURCHED to catch Sloane before she could hit the deck, but the officers' hold kept him on his feet, and she fell to her knees, screaming.

"Let me go," he said. "She needs help."

"The alien ship just incinerated her father's ship," one of the soldiers said, sounding utterly bewildered. Carson, Gareth's brain informed him. The man's name was Carson.

And Carson was clearly delusional. The view screens showed Zander's ship, whole and well. There were no alien ships. There was the wormhole, yes, and the remaining Aemlyn vessels, their intentions unclear. There was also the Current, blinking and storming and sending waves upon waves of thunderous music into his brain. Like drums. Like screeching strings.

There were no aliens.

"Nothing stopping us from firing now," Lager said.

"You're going to hit Zander's ship," Gareth said.

"Remove the Commander from the bridge," Lager repeated. Gareth didn't think he'd ever seen such anger in his friend's eyes. "He is relieved of duty."

Sloane was still on her knees, head buried in her hands. Her scream had given way to silence, her shoulders shaking soundlessly. Gareth tried to shake off the soldiers, but their hold was much too strong as they wrestled him toward the door.

And maybe he ought to let them, he thought. Sloane was weeping, Lager's face a mask of grief. His other officers worked with trembling hands, clearly pulling on their training to keep it together. Like they knew they were headed into battle.

Maybe Sloane was right. The Currents had never sent him images like this—or obscured the truth—but they *were* screaming in his ears. Who knew what they could do—what they *would* do, when up against the feedback of this wormhole?

He stopped fighting, allowing the soldiers to lead him toward the door.

But then Captain Pitorski shoved in front of them, blocking their path to the exit. "Zander's ship is still there," she said, flinging her hand toward the view screen. "The *Starset*. It's not incinerated. There are no other ships, just the ones from Aemlyn."

Gareth let out a breath of relief. He wasn't the only one who knew it. Thank everything.

"It's gone," Sloane sobbed. "You saw what happened, they just—it's gone. They're all gone."

That *wasn't* what they'd seen. But who was right? Carson and his partner had paused, clearly hesitating to push past Pitorski.

And there *was* a way to confirm the *Starset*'s survival. Gareth opened a comm to Zander.

"Why the blushing elephants are *Sabre*'s weapons aimed at me," Sloane's father said, "and why aren't you answering my attempts to hail you?"

Alive. He was definitely alive. Gareth looked to the comms

board, which blinked with attempted hails. Zander's, presumably. The comms officer, who'd replaced Stills after her promotion, sat staring at the board as if he didn't see the lights at all.

"Comms," Gareth said, "broadcast my personal channel."

The Lieutenant twisted in his chair, staring up at Gareth. "There's nothing on your personal channel, sir."

And now Gareth questioned what he could hear. Excellent.

"Oh, for fuck's sake." Ensign Sands hadn't moved from the rail, hadn't given any indication of which version of events he was seeing. Now, he vaulted over the rail, landing on his feet—an impressive maneuver—and then shoved the comms officer out of his seat. Not the route Gareth would've taken, necessarily, but sometimes the blunt approach was called for.

Three officers promptly drew their weapons, but Sands ignored them, punching the button to send Zander's voice into the room.

"Say something, Zander," Gareth said.

"Oh good, you're still there," the man said. "I thought you'd morphed into a plasma cannon. Which is still aimed at me, incidentally. Care to explain?"

He could see where Sloane got her sarcasm. Gareth tried to jerk out of his officers' hold. He needed to reach Sloane, to take her hand, to make her hear what he could hear. If he could just make her understand that what she was seeing wasn't real. He had to believe that it wasn't real.

But Gareth's renewed fighting only strengthened his soldiers' resolve. They moved toward the door once again, ready to push past Pitorski to get him off the bridge. Gareth could only call back over his shoulder. He could only beg her to listen, to trust him. "Your father is alive, Sloane. But if *Sabre* fires, his ship *will* go down."

Sloane just shook her head, tears tracking down her cheeks. If she could hear Zander, she'd be protesting Gareth's removal. She'd be fighting to keep him here.

"They can't see you," Gareth said to Zander. "They can't hear you, either. They see alien ships killing everyone."

"You'd better get them to see us, Commander, or we really will go up in flames."

And it would be *Sabre*'s doing. The Fleet's doing; *his* doing.

He wasn't sure how, though. His soldiers were well trained, holding him firmly under the shoulders. Sands was defending the comms, little good though it would do.

As they reached the doors, Pitorski split away from the rail and threw herself into one of Gareth's guards, knocking him to the ground and jerking Gareth out of the second soldier's grip. Sometimes the blunt approach was called for.

Gareth ran for the rail, but Lager intercepted him. So Gareth punched his friend in the face.

Lager staggered back, and Gareth knew it'd take him mere seconds to recover. So he followed Sands' example, vaulting over the rail and drawing his weapon as he fell. The soldiers should've divested him of that, but they hadn't.

Shouts erupted to every side as he landed, holding his weapon to the nav officer's head. He wasn't at all sure he'd be able to pull the trigger, should it come to that. But if he could bluff his way in, he would. "Abandon your post, Lieutenant," he said.

The officer moved, and Gareth took his spot.

"Where are we going, sir?" Sands asked.

There was no time. None. "Head for the Current," he told Zander, punching in the coordinates.

"When it's having seizures?" Zander asked.

It *was* pulsing like a thunderstorm, both inside his head and out. "There's no choice," Gareth said.

Zander cursed. Gareth had always wondered how bad things

would need to be for him to hear a real curse out of the man. This was it, apparently.

With chaos bubbling around him, hands on his shoulders trying to wrench him out of the chair in spite of his drawn weapon, Gareth pushed the ship into the sizzling Current.

CHAPTER 11

SLOANE HAD BEEN WRONG. *Very* wrong. About as wrong as a person could possibly be and still survive without having killed her entire family.

As soon as *Sabre* hit the Current, the *Starset* had blinked into existence at its side, whole and well and accompanied by her father's voice. Which had been panicked, and swearing real swears, and alive. The word floated through her mind to the rhythm of her heartbeat: alive, alive, alive.

So now Sloane was sitting in the corner of *Sabre*'s cafeteria— 'mess hall,' but she'd never liked that term—sipping tea and missing her coffee and wishing she were in *Moneymaker*'s galley. The cafeteria was too big, too empty. But preferable to sickbay, or a lonely cabin. There were people here, sparse groups of soldiers who were off duty and just as shaken as she was. She didn't want to talk to them, but she wanted to hang out near them. Near-ish.

Sabre probably had a psych department. But it was probably extremely busy right now.

She'd seen her father's ship go up in flames. She'd *seen* it.

Gareth, however, had not.

She felt him enter more than she saw it, felt the soldiers'

spines straighten, the prickle of awareness his proximity sent through her. She kept her eyes on the table, though, even as he sat down across from her and leaned his wrists on the edge, folding his hands and watching her. He didn't say anything. He just sat while she traced a finger along the edge of the table, which was bumpy with raised bolts. Like they just had to make it clear that this was a military ship by giving it ugly tables. She doubted it was any cheaper to keep the bolts exposed.

Obviously, the decor was of the utmost importance and exactly the thing she ought to be focusing on at the moment.

She cleared her throat. It still felt sore from crying and screaming, all that dramatic stuff that'd happened up on the bridge. If she was the kind of person who preferred to dwell in self pity, she'd say she deserved the discomfort. And more.

"I tried to contact Ivy," she said. "To see if she's received more word from Alex through her inlays. No answer."

"She's probably helping Chief Escher to analyze the residue from the stasis field. More important than ever now." His tone was soft, and she heard what he meant, the words he didn't say: *It wasn't your fault. You couldn't have known.* And, worst of all, *Are you all right?*

No. She was not all right.

But he knew better than to say any of that, so he focused on the facts, on executable tasks. The most important of which was Chief Escher's research into the stasis field. Because the only people who'd maintained an accurate view of the situation had been the ones who'd gone through it: Gareth, Sands, and now Pitorski. Who'd accompanied them to the wreck, and therefore been directly exposed to the field.

"It was a mass hallucination," Gareth continued. "The Aemlyn pilots confirmed it."

And they'd killed one of their own ships because of it, just as *Sabre* had almost done to her father's. But Dad and his crew hadn't seen any spiny alien ships or wasp-like fighters. They'd seen what Gareth had seen. They'd seen the truth.

"How come no one on Dad's ship had the hallucination?" she asked.

Gareth just shook his head. He was looking at her too intently, but she kept her own gaze on the table. Easier that way. "We don't know. We only know that no one on the *Starset* experienced the hallucination."

Because it couldn't be neat and clean. No, of course not. On *Sabre*, the three people who'd been immune to this 'mass hallucination' had been through that one particular stasis field out in the bands. The other soldiers who'd been with them there had stayed behind on *Moneymaker* to help Escher. They were probably some of the ones sleeping in Sloane's bed right this second.

The hallucination thing had clearly affected everyone else, convincing the Aemlyn ships to see each other as enemies and prompting mass confusion. Though no doubt Gareth's people would be interviewing everyone who'd been on the Aemlyn ships to check. So why not the *Starset*?

"It wasn't your fault," Gareth said.

And here she'd thought she'd be able to escape without enduring this discussion. She kept her gaze on the table and its stupid bolts, because she still couldn't look at him. Couldn't face him, after failing him like that. See, this was why she needed to stick with useless layabouts like Oliver. Or even a nice but distracted stuckup like Kent. They never hit to the heart of the matter in one sentence.

"I almost killed my entire family," she said. "I was on board with Lager's order. I was okay with removing you from the bridge. How does this end, if we can't even trust that the enemies we see *are* the enemies?"

How did it end, if she couldn't be the leader they all expected her to be?

Gareth just sat there, hands folded on the table. She could see that much of him, at least. He didn't have an answer. And she didn't expect him to.

He couldn't say anything comforting, because there wasn't anything comforting to say. So he wouldn't say anything at all, because he was a nice person and not a lying asshole.

Sloane stood, trying to push her chair back before remembering it was bolted down. "I'm going to get my stuff together so I can get back to *Moneymaker* as soon as we're out of the Current," she said. Brighton had promised to bring the ship close to the Current so they could meet up easily. She was glad she'd asked him for that. She wanted to get back. She wanted to go home.

Gareth stood, too, and she felt more than saw him reach for her. "Sloane—"

Whatever he was going to say, it was interrupted by the arrival of Captain Lager. Who looked as downcast as she felt, his face ashen. Still, he was trying to force a smile, doing his best to recapture some of that upbeat optimism he was so good at. She didn't see what could possibly prompt that, and she was curious enough that she paused, waiting to hear what he had to say.

"It's Hilda," he said. "She's awake."

———

Hilda was sitting up in her bed in the sickbay as Sloane rushed into the room, leaving Gareth and Lager to linger in the doorway. Giving her space, like the nice people they were. They didn't even mention the fact that she was crying.

As Sloane wiped the tears off her cheeks, Hilda rolled her eyes. "Such a baby," she said. "I'm fine. It's just a scratch."

Sloane laughed and sat down on the bed. Hilda was awake; she could give Sloane all the crap she wanted. For at least a day. Maybe even two. "Where's Vin?" she asked.

Hilda made a face, like Sloane had handed her a rotting fish and told her she'd have to eat it if she ever wanted to fly a ship again. "Vin? I haven't seen Vin. Wouldn't want him here, anyway."

Sloane glanced at Gareth before she remembered she'd promised herself she wouldn't look at him. He just shrugged.

She took Hilda's hand, taking a beat to be surprised when the pilot didn't yank it away. They weren't exactly hand holders. "Vin hasn't left your side since you were hurt."

Hilda sniffed, pinching her lips into a tight, disapproving purse. "Then he's a coward who noticed I was waking up and figured he'd better hightail it before I could find my voice and tell him what I think about it."

That... was actually a possibility. "Or," Sloane said, "he thought you might not want to see him."

Hilda waved her away. "I'm awake, you're alive, Vin's a coward, and Striker's using some kind of mass hallucination weapon to control everyone. I'm up to speed."

Sloane looked at Lager. "You let someone *brief* her?"

Lager shrugged. "You try to stop her from getting what she wants."

It was a fair defense.

"The Captain knows what he's about," Hilda said. "So, what next? Throw some officers in that stasis field, make them immune? Then off to save the galaxy?"

If they still could. "Maybe have a sip of water," Sloane suggested. "Rest for a while."

Hilda wrenched her hand away from Sloane's and used it to start fidgeting with the blankets. "I'm rested. I've *been* resting. Now I'm antsy."

"Okay," Sloane said. "I guess we might have to put some officers into the stasis field and make them immune to Striker's hallucinations, yes."

That was a strange sentence. But she was getting used to saying strange sentences.

Before she could say she didn't know what came after that, or how they would get everyone in the entire freaking galaxy into a remote stasis field to protect them from mass hallucinations, her comm chimed with an incoming call from Ivy.

"I'm sorry," she said. "I got your message, but I've been dealing with nonstop transmissions from Alex."

Sloane's heart jumped into her throat. Striker hadn't wrung the wormhole method out of Alex and then had her murdered. Some part of her had been trying to reconcile herself with the possibility. "What's she saying?"

"None of it makes any sense," Ivy said.

"Transmissions?" Hilda asked. "Why isn't Alex on the *Moneymaker*?"

Sloane glanced at Lager. "So you didn't completely brief her."

"She's been awake for less than ten minutes," he protested.

Excuses, excuses. Gareth shot his Captain a look of sympathy, but Lager was avoiding his gaze, too. When it was Lager doing it, it did seem a little silly. His fault or not, though, it was a big mistake to recover from. Sloane might not have been protesting Lager's order to fire, but Lager would have been the one giving it. That'd weigh on him. How could it not?

Not to mention the fact that he'd tried to relieve his Commander from duty.

Sloane returned her attention to Hilda. Who was glaring at her, clearly unhappy with the lag in response time. "Striker kidnapped Alex," Sloane explained. "She'd communicating with Ivy through the inlays."

Hilda made a sound of disgust. "Alex would *never* make a wormhole for that snake."

Sloane said. "Only she did. She *is*. Ivy? Can you tell us what the transmissions say?"

There was a long pause. "Maybe it'll be better if I can project them to you. And um... I think you'd better make sure the Commander's there. He needs to see this."

CHAPTER 12

IT TOOK ALL of ten minutes to mobilize the group to the nearest conference room. Most of which was spent watching as Sloane bullied the doctor into letting his newly awakened patient leave the sickbay at all. The doctor had tried to appeal to Gareth, revealing a skewed understanding of how much power his Commander actually had.

Which, in this case, was very little. Gareth watched as Sloane ignored the doctor's protests and transferred Hilda's monitors and IV over to a mobile cart with a swiftness that suggested well-honed muscle memory. He doubted she realized how skilled she actually was, handling medical equipment like she'd just left the academy yesterday.

She must have called Vin, because he was waiting in the conference room when they arrived, leaning against the wall, his eyes glued to the center of the room as if awaiting the presentation. And determined not to look Hilda's way. With Sloane and Lager avoiding Gareth's gaze, he wasn't sure how anyone would be able to look anywhere. Even if Sloane did seem marginally better than she had in the mess hall, where she'd been huddled over her untouched mug of tea, shoulders hunched, as forlorn as he'd ever seen her.

And then Ivy was on the comm, and everyone looked expectantly toward the table. Whatever she had to say, it was important. "The transmissions are confused," Ivy said by way of a greeting. "I'm not sure Alex even knows she's broadcasting them. But she's been sending this."

The projector flared to life, and Sloane gasped in recognition as the Fleet Tower appeared. It was unmistakable, with its tiered landing platforms jutting out at regular intervals. Gareth's breath squeezed out of his lungs at the sight of it, and he found himself leaning closer, as if he might catch a glimpse of a friend.

Or, more likely, someone who'd turned against him. As far as he knew, everyone who was left at the Fleet Tower still believed him to be a traitor—or, worse, they believed in Striker's mission and wanted to defeat him as he was.

The image zoomed in closer, then flickered, and the Fleet Tower blinked out of sight. Something about the suddenness of the shifting images made Gareth think of a dream. Strange and stuttering, and following some hidden logic that might or might not be revealed.

The new view showed workers hauling a collection of huge bars through the halls. He didn't know how else to describe them; he might have thought they were steel beams, had they not been studded with grids of lights and controls. Some kind of technology, but he couldn't place it. Perhaps because it'd been dismantled.

Another zoom, another flicker, and the workers were hefting the bars to stand upright in the center of an open warehouse of a room. He recognized the space, though he'd never seen it empty like this. It was part of the Fleet's tech vault.

"They're wormhole stabilizers," Ivy explained. "According to the transmissions, they're being kept in the Fleet's tech vault."

"We don't have wormhole stabilizers," Gareth said, throat dry. There were, as he'd learned, quite a few things he didn't know about Fane and the Fleet Tower. His mother's secret passageways, for one. But he'd made it a point to know the contents of the tech vaults. They were kept in the most secure section of the most secure building in the galaxy. The Commander damn well ought to know what they contained.

"They're moving the stabilizers *in*," Sloane said. The images were flashing between the exterior view of the tower, then the tunnel, then the warehouse. Pointed enough. Gareth squinted at the pictures, trying to draw out the details, trying to figure out why Alex would communicate with them this way.

"Maybe she's trying to tell us her wormholes are stabilized," Gareth said. Though that still didn't explain why the scientist would agree to make them for Striker.

"That's what I thought," Ivy said. "So I talked to Amayra. She said the Interplanetary Dwellers have seen drawings of stabilizers like this. They call them gateways. But they're like a myth, something we... something the Interplanetary Dwellers have searched for but never found."

"So they've been found," Sloane said. "It was bound to happen, right?"

Ivy made a sound that might have been agreement or confusion. "Maybe. But she also said she wouldn't have expected them to be movable. They're a place *and* a technology, woven together."

Or so the Interplanetary Dwellers thought. They knew a lot about this alien technology, it was true, but they were only experts because they knew more than everyone else.

In actuality, they might know very little.

"I hate to say this," Hilda said, "but would Alex be willing to work for Striker if he had the means to get her life's work back? Wormholes stabilized. Problem solved."

Except for the small matter of helping to create a galactic empire.

"No," Ivy said immediately. "She wouldn't."

According to Sloane, the scientist had been devastated when she'd learned she couldn't safely continue her work. Gareth wasn't sure what imploding the universe meant, specifically, only that it was undeniably a very, very bad thing. The grating song of the Current agreed.

The Current was allowing them to pass through it, for now. To Gareth, it felt unstable. Ready to blow.

Silence. A tap of fingernails on the table. Under it, perhaps; he couldn't see who was doing the tapping. Vin looked thoughtful, one finger pressed to his bottom lip, and Gareth found himself wondering about his read on the question. He'd crewed with Alex for a while before Sloane took over.

"I don't believe Alex would create wormholes for the enemy," Sloane said finally. "She takes them too seriously. She knows the damage he could do."

But the truth of the matter was that someone had opened a wormhole. And that Alex was the only person, at least in this galaxy, with the ability to do it. They couldn't get around that.

"Alex might help Striker," Gareth said, "if he threatened all of you."

More silence. Sloane wedged her lower lip between her teeth, and Hilda gave her loose hair an absentminded tug, then startled in confusion as if she'd expected to find it braided. "Okay," she said. "Let's say Alex is creating the wormhole. Which she wouldn't do without this stabilizer thing, no matter what he threatened, because imploding the universe would be bad for all of us. But if she *is* using the stabilizer thing, then why's the Current freaking out?"

In Gareth's head, the Current's song screeched in agreement.

When Sloane looked at Hilda, eyebrows raised, the pilot just said, "I didn't need debriefing on that part. The ship *has* windows. It's like a lightning storm out there. I'm surprised it hasn't microwaved us all by now."

They could make all the guesses they wanted. Unless they spoke directly to Alex, they had no way of knowing exactly what the transmissions were telling them. But they did need to take action, and they needed to do it soon.

"I think we have to believe she's sending the messages for a reason," Sloane said. "It's the only starting point we have. Besides, it'd probably be a good idea to take back Fane."

An afterthought to her. A central problem for the Fleet. Gareth looked at Lager, in part because he couldn't help but wonder what the Captain would do if addressed directly. "What do you think?"

Lager had his hands tucked in the small of his back. He hadn't relaxed his stance since the meeting began. "She's got a point, sir."

This was the kind of informal meeting during which Gareth would expect Lager to take on a more casual role. He was an expert strategist, and he was a friend. He was watching closely, but his mouth was set in an unusually solemn line. There was a bruise starting to form on his cheek where Gareth had hit him.

Sloane stood. "Fane it is. As soon as we exit the Current, I'm going back to my ship."

"I'm coming, too," Hilda said.

"Like hell," Sloane replied. "You need to stay here with the doctors."

"Try and make me."

The door closed behind the women, muting their argument, and Vin followed them, making a comment under his breath about going with them so they wouldn't kill each other. As willful as they both were, Gareth didn't know who to place bets on. They'd work it out, though likely only after an hour of bickering.

Lager made to follow them, but Gareth rested a hand on his friend's arm. "Martin. A moment, if you have it."

Lager paused, snapping back to that too-stiff attention. Honestly, a statue of a Fleet soldier would have moved more. "Sir," he said, "when this is over, I want to tender my—"

"Don't say it," Gareth interrupted.

"Sir." Lager hesitated. Wet his lips. Drew in a long breath. "You need commanding officers who think clearly."

Lager wasn't usually the type to put everything on himself like this. But the situation was extreme by any measure, and it was an instinct that Gareth understood well enough. "It was pure luck that you were affected and I wasn't," he said. "I do not accept your resignation."

Lager pressed his lips together, as if caught between the desire to pay for his mistakes and the need to follow Gareth's orders. After a second, he relented. "Yes, sir."

"And I apologize for punching you," Gareth said.

Finally, Lager smiled. "You've got a good right hook, sir."

"Will you please stand at ease? You're making me nervous."

Lager obeyed, but his smile was still tentative. Like he expected a left hook to follow.

"Did you have something else to add?" Gareth asked. "Any ideas, now that we're on the same page?"

Lager shook out his arms, like he was dispelling the last of the concrete that'd been holding him at attention. He leaned his hands on the table, looking at the still-flickering images of the Fleet Tower. "We should stop at Lostelle on the way," he said. "There's one person who knows Fane better than you."

"There's quite a few, I'd wager," Gareth murmured. "Haven't spent much time there in recent years."

He'd never been much for offices.

"Which is why we need an expert," Lager said. "*The* expert, really."

Understanding hit him like a breaker crashing against the sand. "Oh, no."

"Yes, sir," Lager said, grinning in earnest now. "We're going to need to pick up your mother."

CHAPTER 13

THE INSIDES of Sloane's eyelids felt sandy, along with the inside of her brain. Which was very disappointed to be sitting at yet another conference table in front of yet another presentation. Still on *Sabre*. Not on *Moneymaker*. Where her bed was familiar and coffee was available, at least for a few more brews.

"Are we really going to go over more hologram plans?" she asked, leaning back in her chair. It didn't scoot very far, probably to prevent upstarts like her from propping their feet up on the table. Which was a good idea, since that was her inclination at the moment. "I'm starting to get confused."

Gareth was seated beside her. He didn't look nearly as tired as she felt, at least from what she could see out of the corner of her eye. Maybe he'd actually managed to get some sleep, without the guilt of having almost firing on the *Starset* to weigh him down. He leaned toward her, his shoulder brushing against hers as if begging her to meet his eye. "The diagrams are supposed to help you *not* be confused," he said.

Sloane sighed. "And yet."

The guest list had grown since their last hologram party. Hilda and Vin were still there, though Captain Lager had returned to the bridge to do ship-running things. When they'd reached Lostelle, Dad had transferred over from the *Starset* so he could be involved in the conversation, for unknown reasons. He didn't know Fleet Tower any better than Sloane did; in fact, she'd traveled its secret passages, and he hadn't. Not that it was a competition. Except that it was, a little.

And, of course, there was Candace. She stood at the head of the table, the crinkle in her forehead broadcasting her annoyance with all of them. Also for unknown reasons.

"Quiet," she said, though Sloane hadn't complained for at least ten seconds. "We have limited time, because you insisted on coming to pick me up when this entire conversation could have been a text communication."

Sloane didn't disagree, but no one had asked her. Probably for the best that the Fleet officers had decided.

Candace flicked her wrist, and a too-familiar image of Fleet Tower materialized in front of them. "Director West found our secret passages and shut them down," she said. "All, we think, except for one."

"We *think*?" Sloane asked. It seemed like the kind of detail you should be absolutely certain about before basing big, heisty plans on it.

Candace ignored her. She pinched her fingers, expanding the details of a floor in the middle of the tower. A blinking red line ran up the side of the tower like a vein, the projected map following it down into a utility tunnel. Too bad it didn't come with an exit to the tech vault. There'd been one of those passages before, though it'd probably been blocked early. Too many people knew about it.

Dad's dark eyes were sharp as he watched the hologram, as if he thought he could jump into it and enter Fleet Tower from here if only he concentrated hard enough. "Why didn't they find it?"

"It's special," Candace replied.

"Special how?" Sloane asked.

"What if they *did* find it?" Dad asked.

Gareth shifted, and she could practically feel his amusement. If Vin chimed in next, he was probably going to start laughing. Too many Tarnishes in one room, or something.

"Then the fighting will start sooner than we want it to," Candace replied.

"Special *how?*" Sloane repeated, raising her voice slightly.

"All right," Dad said.

Sloane waved her hand in the projection, scattering the light. "Can you hear me? Or did someone finally manage to put me on mute?"

"We hear you, dear," Candace said. "Sit down."

Sloane sat, letting herself lean toward Gareth before she remembered she was trying to keep her distance. "Our families are getting along great already."

Now he *did* laugh.

"We get in through the tunnel," Candace said. "We kidnap West, and we use his credentials to access the tech vault. Then we look for the gateways."

Gareth was frowning, his hands splayed on the table. "And when you say 'we,' you mean..."

Candace was already heading for the door. "Get out of my way," she said. "I'm going to need some armor."

———

No one seemed to believe Sloane when she'd said she could only stare at holo plans for a limited time before losing her mind. Eventually, she decided to leave without permission. They could fill her in. Or not.

She'd been hoping to take a snack break in peace, and was on the verge of choosing between potato chips and a chocolate bar—

at least *Sabre* had decent snacks—when Gareth materialized beside her, appearing so suddenly and silently that she was pretty sure he'd snuck up on her intentionally.

Not a bad plan, when her first inclination was to take off running in the other direction. She should've figured he'd come to find her eventually.

"I recommend the chocolate," he said.

Sloane took the chips, then changed her mind and snagged both. She was going to need the sustenance for the ground mission. And for this conversation too, probably.

Snack acquired, she turned to run, but Gareth caught her hand and pulled her back a step. He'd let her go if she pushed. But she couldn't quite bring herself to do that.

"Lager already tried to resign," he said. "I won't accept yours either."

"Maybe you want to resign," she said. "From... being with me."

Knowing him, he'd submit a formal application to dump her as soon as they'd saved the galaxy. He'd provide copies in triplicate, everything neat and tidy.

She hadn't quite realized that was a concern until she said it.

Gareth pulled her a step closer. "Will you look at me?"

"Nope."

"Sloane."

She sighed. They were about to storm his home planet together, take back the Fleet Tower, and possibly die in the process. If there was one thing she'd learned from going into so many possibly-we'll-die situations lately, it was that she hated to do it with anything left unresolved.

So she looked at him. "I'm sorry," she said. "I'm sorry I didn't believe you, and I'm sorry I was going to let Lager relieve you from duty."

She wasn't sure what she could have done to stop him with

all those soldiers there. But Pitorski had done her part. Sloane hadn't believed in him. She'd made the wrong call.

"You thought you saw your family murdered in front of your eyes," he said gently.

She could still see the explosion when she closed them. It had looked so real. So very real. "You know the worst part? The look of disgust on Lissie's face when she saw me. Like I was less than nothing to her. The only thing I could think, when I thought they might be gone, was that I'd let her down again."

Gareth touched his lips briefly to hers. "Come on," he said. "Let's go make it right."

CHAPTER 14

GARETH HADN'T BEEN LIVING ALL that long with the knowledge of his mother's secret spy career. What her mission was, or who employed her, or how many people she had working for her... all mysteries. The extent of his knowledge boiled down to a network of operatives, quite a few secret tunnels, and thus-far-unrevealed methods for obtaining knowledge that no one else had.

Because this was all new to him, there was something distinctly unnerving about watching his mother parachute to Fane's surface with a squad of soldiers and a handful of bots, but she wore her Fleet armor like a second skin, handling the parachute like an expert. She could've schooled a few of his soldiers in better technique. Hell, she could have schooled *him*.

Sloane and Ivy were dropping with them, too, having left Hilda to fly *Moneymaker* and Vin to watch over her. Brighton was assisting Chief Escher in the lab in Ivy's absence. Which she'd essentially demanded, especially after Gareth ordered her assistants back to *Sabre*. It was too dangerous to concentrate all the stasis field experts in one place.

They came down in a drop field that was concealed in the

center of an orchard several miles from the city. Tucked within a pocket of Fleet housing, the trees were in full bloom, the grass already littered with white and pink petals. Using the trees for cover, they moved through the neighborhood from behind, passing rows of fenced-off backyards. The houses here were neat and tidy, as if the dwellings were expected to stand at attention, their uniforms crisp and unsullied. Beige paint, blue shutters, neutral curtains. Everything crisp and identical, comfortable and clean.

Not at all like the neighborhood Gareth had grown up in, where the gardens were wilder, the grass taller, and you were more likely to find a werewolf than a gnome guarding the zinnias. Or so he'd pretended as a child.

Despite his family's Fleet lifestyle, it'd always fit.

As his mother led them along the fence, Gareth wondered how many families came to pick apples and jump in hay piles here, never knowing it was a base for secret operations. Not that he could think of the last time it'd been used as such under his watch.

Before long, Mom led them through a gap in the fence and up to the rear of a small rectangular building. He could see the edge of a sign peeking up from the other side, but he couldn't read it. Mom opened a panel next to the door—he'd have sworn it was a regular brick, just like the rest—and punched in a few numbers. The door popped open, and they shuffled inside.

It was a tight fit between a glassed-in counter to the left and a pastel wallpapered wall to the right. The place smelled like sugar.

"It's an ice cream shop," Sloane said, peering into the counter. He wondered what his mother would do if she made herself a cone.

Thankfully, she didn't. Mom moved behind the counter and knelt, knees popping, to pull a rug away from a trapdoor. A quick twist of the key, and the panel opened to reveal a brick of solid concrete.

No passage. No ladder.

"They found it," Sloane said. "It's filled in."

Gareth's mind was already running to Plan B, trying to calculate how close they could get to the city before they'd be detected. West was a traitor, but he wasn't a fool. He'd be a fool if he'd loosened any of the Tower's security. He'd be watching.

Still crouched beside the door, Mom grinned and brushed a stray lock of gray hair out of her face. She liked this secret agent stuff. That was clear enough. She leaned down, ran her fingers along the edge of the box, and pulled a lever.

The concrete *twisted*. And then it blinked away, revealing a ladder that descended into a dark hole. Gareth wondered if the shop owner knew this existed.

"It's a hologram," Mom said, starting down onto the ladder.

"Now you're just showing off," Sloane said, but she was beaming, too. Definitely impressed.

Pitorski, who never would have let Gareth drop into a secret passage ahead of her, allowed his mother to lead the way before calling the bots and two members of her squad forward to clear the area. Gareth and Sloane followed, with Ivy and the bots behind them, the final pair of squad members taking up the rear.

The not-concrete panel slid into place behind them, leaving them in a tunnel with dim red lighting and walls that suddenly felt much too narrow. Not that he was claustrophobic. He just preferred the roomy width of a ship's corridors.

Pitorski took the lead without asking permission, and Mom seemed content to let her do it. She fell back to walk with Gareth.

"Interplanetary Dwellers' tech?" he asked, tipping his head toward the trap door and the illusion.

"No," she said. "*Our* tech."

He wanted more than expected her to elaborate. He could

almost feel Sloane listening, though she was walking behind them. She'd want to hear the explanation, too. Instead of giving them one, Mom let the question hang: 'who's *us*?'

But Gareth didn't ask it. He just kept walking, scanning the tunnel ahead, listening to his soldiers' footfalls and Sloane's breathing behind him, the bots' wheels rumbling along the dirt floor.

"You want the Fleet to have oversight," Mom said finally. "To answer to someone. It's noble, the way you're arranging the Systems into a friendly little coalition. But who's going to oversee the overseers?"

He supposed he shouldn't be surprised that she knew about the meeting. Even without her secret spy network, she'd have heard about it from the leaders who were hiding out on Lostelle.

"They oversee each other," Gareth replied. "That's the point."

Mom coughed, like the dust was getting to her. It scratched at his throat, too. "In theory. But there's no recourse, is there? Just peer pressure. Domer's laws don't apply on Schere. King Lebnil can't force anything on Elter. It's all just... a hope. And it'll crumble with the first corrupt member. As you saw with Osmond."

Gareth grimaced. He still felt like he'd failed Osmond Clay, somehow. "So you're what," he said, "assassins? Enforcers?"

She smacked him on the arm. "Don't be crude. We're problem solvers."

How did they solve those problems, though? Through what means? He wanted to know—and he also didn't want to know. Not that she'd tell him, anyway.

"All right," he said. "But who signs your paychecks?"

She didn't answer. He didn't expect her to. For a while, it was just footsteps and Pitorski's occasional reassurances that they were clear, sensor readings clear, visuals clear. The tunnel smelled like dirt and sugar, like Mom's operatives had spent years tracking ice cream back here. Spies, stopping in for a treat before their next operation.

Some of which must have been to spy on her husband's people. Gareth tried to imagine how his father would have responded to that. Part of him was fairly certain that Dad would have been impressed. And maybe not all that shocked, in the end.

"I'm getting old for this, Gareth," Mom said.

Gareth looked at her, surprised. She navigated this secret world so easily, seemed to enjoy it. No; remembering that grin on her face, the self-satisfied way she'd revealed the hologram, he was *sure* she enjoyed it.

"I know," she said, winking. "I look thirty."

"Not a day past," he said.

"I want to retire," she went on. "I want to get a bunch of cats and teach them to fetch."

"I think that's dogs."

"I want cats that fetch," she said. "This job? I could trust it to you. It's right up Sloane's alley, too, don't you think?"

He was pretty sure that Mom could get Sloane's reaction to that suggestion just by turning around, since she'd almost certainly been listening to their entire conversation. But Mom didn't turn, and Sloane didn't say anything.

And before he had time to think of a response, the passage ended. As his mother, who knew these tunnels so well, must have intended. She patted him on the shoulder, right in the spot where she'd hit him a few minutes ago. "Think on it, dear," she said. "Plenty of action. None of the politics."

And then she was following Pitorski up a long set of stairs, pushing ahead where he'd have preferred she let him go first. At least she let the squad precede her up the stairs as the walls shifted to metal plating, the passage narrowing even further so that they had no choice but to ascend in single file. Every now and then, he could hear the bots scraping against the walls as they used their hovering capabilities to float up the steps.

It was hard not to imagine that this tunnel must have been put in place to begin with, designed right along with the original tower. Perhaps he could find some answers on Mom's organization if he followed the trail back to the person who'd designed it in the first place. Or the one who'd served as Commander at the time.

"I hate spiral staircases," Sloane muttered.

"It's not a spiral," he said. "More like a switchback."

"Same idea. Too much narrow. Too much up. My stomach doesn't like it."

His didn't, either. But they were wedged in now, with only one way to go.

Gareth had been neglecting his physical fitness regimens, what with all the galactic takeover distractions, and he wasn't sorry when they reached the landing. Pitorski arranged a soldier on either side of the door, then gestured for one of them to pull the latch to open it.

A sliver of fluorescent light cracked into the stairs, widening into a beam.

And then they were looking straight into the barrel of a Fleet-class astral fusion rifle.

Behind him, Sloane groaned. "Great. Turns out it *is* guarded."

CHAPTER 15

SLOANE DIDN'T LIKE this game.

Nothing was ever easy. Nothing happened the way it should. And now, they were probably about to be captured by Striker's number-one ally. Not the best day.

The guard at the top of the stairs ushered Pitorski out of the stairwell, and a second one divested her of her weapons. Same with the next two soldiers. And if trained soldiers couldn't hold on to their guns, Sloane didn't see how she had any hope of keeping hers.

As Gareth stepped into the light, though, the moment shifted.

The guard's eyes widened, and he lowered his weapon, swiftly gesturing to his buddy to do the same. "Commander," he said. "You're alive."

Relief. The expression on his face was shock, and pure relief.

"Yes," Gareth said carefully. "And you are?"

Sloane was aware that he was attempting to fill the doorway, to act as a shield, lowered weapons or not. Joke was on him, because if he got shot then he'd fall back and knock both Sloane and Candace down this awful staircase. Which would not end well for them.

And then she heard it. The rattle of gunfire in the background, the sizzle-and-burn of plasma hitting walls. The Fleet Tower was a war zone. And she hadn't even started it this time.

Sloane went up on her tiptoes and peeked over Gareth's shoulder, earning herself an exasperated look from Candace as she squeezed in beside the older woman. "Ooh," she said, "are you guys doing an uprising?"

The soldier nodded and stepped further into the corridor, allowing Gareth into the hall as his friends handed the squad's weapons back to them. He had spiky blond hair and a gap between his top front teeth. It made him look younger than he probably was. "Took time to piece it together," he said. "But we saw what Striker did, locking Ilya and Halorin up in those shields."

He seemed indignant at the idea that Striker could have fooled them into following the CTF for long. "West won't budge," he added, "so we figured we should take Fane back ourselves. Sir."

Gareth clapped the guard on the shoulder, his smile matching his soldier's relief. Sloane knew how much it'd been weighing on him, fighting his own people. "Well done, soldier. What's your name?"

"I'm Lieutenant Farley," the gap-toothed guard said. "This is Stokes and Hart. But almost everyone's on your side, sir. It's us against the CTF now. And West."

He said West's name like a curse, like he needed to spit it out to keep from getting sick. Sloane noted, with satisfaction, that he'd stripped the Director title, too.

"Well done," Gareth said again. "We're here for West. We need his access to the tech vaults."

Lieutenant Farley nodded. "On it, sir."

And they were. The soldiers escorted them through the halls, making quick work of any would-be ambushers. It didn't hurt that the CTF had decided to identify themselves by wearing their pretty black arm bands. Sloane couldn't help but wonder where Striker had even found all these people. So many of them, willing to die to defend his would-be empire. What lies did they believe?

She kept her own shooter ready, but she didn't even need to fire it. The soldiers formed a shield around the group, their battle armor protecting against periodic shots that pinged through their section of the hallways. She could hear more fighting in the distance, sounding much worse than it was here, but that might have been the echoey nature of the halls. The place smelled like burning plastic, the walls sporting occasional dents and splotches of char. How long had this been going on? Since Striker had enclosed Ilya, or close to it. At least based on what Farley had said.

She'd known for a while that the Fleet wasn't as incompetent as she'd once assumed. Even so, this was impressive. It wasn't easy to organize a resistance, especially with the barrage of misinformation that'd been hammering them from all sides. Not easy at all.

When they reached Gareth's office—West's office now, though Gareth didn't really seem to care—the door was locked.

"Anyone know a code?" Gareth asked.

He was looking at Candace, who shrugged innocently.

Farley, however, aimed his gun at the control panel. Definitely the same code Sloane would have suggested.

Before he could shoot, though, the copper bot whirred in from behind, knocking Sloane aside in its rush to reach the door. It'd been uncharacteristically quiet until now. And apparently didn't think it was 'wont to lose consciousness,' or whatever excuse it'd used not to retrieve the shield controls back on Ve Station.

The copper bot threw itself between the gun and the wall, as if to save a friend from disembowelment. "Finesse," it said, "is preferable to violence."

It stopped in front of the door, popped open a panel in its sort-of abdomen area, and shot out a long prod with a circular module at the end. Which it promptly stuck into the door control panel. Sloane didn't even know where the circular module was supposed to fit—there weren't any visible ports—but the bot just rested the module against the console.

Nothing happened.

"Faster to shoot it out, sir," Farley said.

"Finesse," the copper bot repeated.

"And how long does finesse take?" Gareth asked.

The door popped open, and the copper bot wheeled itself back with a distinctly satisfied air. "No time at all."

"At least it's modest," Sloane said.

Sloane entered just in time to catch a satisfying view of Pitorski as she hauled Director West ass-first out of the secret passageway that led into this office, the one through which Candace had first surprised them when West and Striker had ambushed them here. Ah, memories.

West kicked like a captured rat, his glasses askew as the soldiers hauled him to his feet. Once they clapped magna cuffs around his wrists, though, all the fight went out of him. His shoulders slumped, his hair a mess of frizzy tangles.

One piece down. One piece to go.

Sloane didn't think better of West for dropping the struggle as they hauled him down to the tech vaults. She'd have respected a good fight more than this sad resignation. But she supposed she couldn't complain about the lack of trouble.

Or at least, it was the minimum amount of trouble they could have expected, with the whole place engaged in hallway combat. West came along with the docility of a captured coward, and Farley was able to escort them via the elevators. Which was a good thing, given that Sloane's thighs were screaming at her for the tower-ascending workout from hell.

"You're holding the tech vault," Gareth said to Farley as the elevator pulled to a stop. He sounded impressed.

Farley and Pitorski exited, made sure the guards were theirs, then beckoned the group forward. They were working well together, for soldiers who'd only just met. Then again, they were both Fleet trained. Probably had protocols and things.

"Important stuff down here, sir," Farley replied. "Gotta protect it."

"Who's in charge of the resistance?" Gareth asked. "Is it you?"

Sloane wondered if he'd thought to question whether a resistance leader could be a threat in and of themselves. But that was just the cynic in her talking. Sometimes, good things just... happened.

Not often. But sometimes.

Farley shook his head. "It's you, sir. This is just... a group effort."

Gareth swallowed, looking distinctly verklempt. He turned to greet the new band of loyal Fleet soldiers, while Pitorski scanned the area, alert. Candace was crossing her arms like she was late for an appointment and they were all holding her up with all their reunions and feelings and such.

As for West, the weaselly intelligence director—*former* director—was huddled between two of Pitorski's soldiers, his shoulders raised as if he hoped to will them into swelling up and swallowing him whole. Like a turtle. Or a snake, diving back into its hole.

Sloane paced closer to him, tilting her head to look him in the eye. Not easy, since he was decidedly avoiding her gaze. "Where did Striker bring the gateways?" she asked. "Which vault?"

West looked up, damp tangles of hair falling into his face. "What?"

"The wormhole stabilizers," she said. "Where are they?"

West was shaking his head, sending little rivers of sweat trickling down his cheeks. "The gateways aren't here. What are you going to do to me?"

But his answer told her much more than he seemed to realize. Number one, that the gateways did exist. And two, that West knew about them. Otherwise, he'd be looking at her with even more confusion than he was now. He was, Sloane considered, a terrible spy.

Ivy slipped through from the back of the group, making her way past soldiers and bots alike. "I saw them here," she said. "In one of the vaults. You have to tell us which one."

West made a strangled noise in the back of his throat, then coughed. "You sound just like him," he said. "He's riding me for intel I don't have. Just because he knows what they look like doesn't mean I can summon the things out of thin air. The galaxy is *huge*."

Sloane looked at Gareth. "He is the whiniest Fleet officer I've ever met."

Gareth shook his head. "And I was the one who hired him."

Sloane let her eyes wander down the hall, where the soldiers were arranged in a cluster in the center, weapons lowered but muscles primed to leap into action in the event of attack. The tech vault was actually a series of vaults, with doors stationed at lockstep intervals, each with control panels and wheelie locks that even the copper bot would have trouble opening.

"Striker doesn't know where the stabilizers are," she said slowly.

"That's what I'm *saying* to you," West said. "I don't have the personnel to search the entire—"

"But he's feeding Alex a hallucination," Sloane interrupted. West was useless. She didn't care what he had to say. "So she thinks the wormholes she's making for Striker are stabilized. He just chose Fane as his stage."

Gareth nodded, considering. "It would make sense for him to bring them here."

How the hallucination weapon thing worked, she had no idea. She didn't want to. But Striker knew Fane, and he knew Fleet Tower. If he could feed images to it, they might well be believable enough, even for someone who'd walked these halls.

And if he could feed any images through it, he could convince Alex her friends were in danger with what she'd see as solid evidence. The alien ships coming out of that second wormhole had looked so real, the *Starset*'s explosion so final. Sloane had a feeling she'd be having nightmares about it for years to come. Maybe forever.

"The gateways exist, and they're somewhere in the Parse Galaxy," Sloane said. "Somewhere we can find."

West was quivering and dripping sweat on the floor, looking like he might vomit on her shoes at any second. She took a step back, but she kept her attention on him. "What do we know about the gateways?" she asked. "How does Striker know what they look like?"

West was getting paler by the second. "I don't know. He doesn't tell me things."

Sloane wondered if growling would get more information out of him. Probably not. She looked at Farley. "How many soldiers in this tower want to string the former director up by his toes?"

Farley studied West. "I'd say all of them."

"All right, I'll hand him over to you," she said. "Since he clearly doesn't know anything else."

"Okay." West held up a trembling hand. "Okay, he said he saw them in some Interplanetary Dwellers' text. Something he managed to hold on to after you took their tech back. An actual book, with ink and paper."

"Like Damian's book," Gareth said.

The one the pirate had stolen after they freed him from prison, then spent weeks poring over like it contained the secrets of the universe. Or at least a very good chili recipe. Sloane had ever seen obsessing over a paper book like that. Probably a different book, but if they both belonged to the Interplanetary Dwellers, then they'd have one thing in common.

"An alien book," Sloane said.

Damn Damian for disappearing. Even if he had saved them all in the process.

"If Striker found pictures of these gateways in the alien book, then they're from another part of the galaxy," Sloane said.

"Obviously," West coughed.

Sloane ignored him. "Where do we know for sure that someone with mysterious powers had a foothold in our part of the galaxy?"

"Adu System," Ivy breathed. "Sever."

The deposed tyrant, back to haunt them once again. Somehow, it seemed impossible that the gateways could be anywhere *but* Adu. It was inevitable; they should have started there in the first place. And it would occur to Striker eventually, too. No way it wouldn't.

"Narrows it down," Gareth said, "but it's still an entire star system."

Sloane stepped around West to where the three bots were still waiting inside the elevator. "Can you search Adu for technology, if we provide holo images of it?"

The copper bot quivered, its plate-hat rattling like a boiling teapot. "Of course," it said. It sounded offended. "The primary calling, the sacred task handed to us by our makers, makes us hunters. Whether we wish to hunt or not." It hummed, turning a slow circle. "Makers. Makes. There's something there, don't you think?"

Something ridiculous, Sloane thought, but she only nodded. No need to antagonize the bots. "Good," she said. "Personally, I think we should start with the Hold."

CHAPTER 16

GARETH COULD REMEMBER A TIME, not very long ago, when Sloane had seen her ship only as a burden. So eager to get rid of it, and so determined to get back to a life she hadn't even wanted. She'd barely been able to find engineering when he'd first met her, and she'd had no desire to.

Now, she beamed up at *Moneymaker* like it was the most beautiful ship in the entire galaxy as the beat-up old freighter descended onto the Fleet Tower's roof. Her grin was as wide as he'd ever seen it, even as the wind whipped her hair into a frenzy of tangles, forcing her to keep flipping it back over her shoulder and out of her face. Gareth wouldn't be surprised if she ran forward and kissed the hull as soon as the ship touched the landing pad.

Well. There *were* plenty of reasons to celebrate.

Gareth turned to Lieutenant Farley, who was guarding the entrance back into the Tower with Captain Pitorski at his side. The two seemed to be settling into an easy partnership, their training making it easy to find common ground, though Pitorski was still watching the Lieutenant with an edge of wariness. It was understandable enough, given the recent uncertainties about who was actually on which side. They'd work it out soon enough.

"I'm leaving you two in joint command," he said. "We need Pitorski here at the Tower, in case Striker attacks with his mass-hallucination weapon."

There hadn't been much time to brief Farley and the others on that unfortunate new development, but it was among the most crucial information they had to relay. If Striker aimed that weapon at them, he'd be able to snatch the Tower back up in no time, and free West from his jail cell. The soldiers wouldn't even know which side they'd aided until it was too late.

"Captain Pitorski is immune to the hallucinations," he continued, "so trust her version of things. No matter how strange it seems."

Farley nodded, back straight, eyes scanning the skies dutifully. Gareth didn't love the idea of leaving Pitorski behind—he relied on her, and often—but Fleet Tower needed at least one officer who could see past Striker's lies. At least until they could get more soldiers to the bands.

Not an easy proposition. Their ships were spread thin enough as it was, and he'd already sent Captain Peters and the *Bayonet* out to take a swim in the stasis field. One frigate already felt like too many. Had to be done.

Gareth shook Farley's hand as *Moneymaker* settled onto the landing pad with a series of clinks and clanks that made the Lieutenant's eyes widen. "Don't worry," Gareth said. "It's normal."

In fact, it sounded significantly less worrisome with Hilda at the helm than it did when almost anyone else was flying—including himself. Like it refused to perform at its best for anyone else.

Farley still seemed concerned, but Gareth gave him one last nod, then headed for the ship. As soon as the gangplank hit the landing pad, Sloane surged toward it, meeting Brighton halfway up with a high five.

A victory, among so many losses. It was well worth a celebration.

Ivy, however, lagged behind Sloane, her lips rolled together in worry. And no wonder. Had Striker been holding Sloane instead of Alex, Gareth would have found it impossible to celebrate any victory, large or small, until she was back in his arms.

They still had to free Alex; they still had a war to win. But victories were always good for morale, so Gareth let himself smile as he joined the rest of the crew in heading up the gangplank.

"I wanted to bake cupcakes!" BRO announced as Gareth stepped into the cargo bay. "Zander says the *Starset* has sugar! I wanted to get some! But then I remembered I don't have hands."

Gareth's mother, who'd followed him up the gangplank in uncharacteristic silence, was shaking her head. "Strangest AI I've ever met," she said.

"Thank you!" BRO sounded genuinely pleased. "I'm sorry about the cupcakes, though."

"Space cupcakes never taste right, anyway," Mom said.

"That's comforting!" BRO replied. "I like you!"

Mom gave her head another shake, then made for the stairs that led up to the main part of the ship. "I'll transfer over to *Sabre* as soon as we're out of atmo."

"More shadows to hide in?" Gareth asked, before he could stop himself. He hadn't expected her to stay on *Moneymaker* for long. In fact, it was something of a surprise that she didn't have her own extraction worked out.

She shot him a look. "You say it like you're kidding, but I know you're not. Think about my offer, Gareth. It's a limited time one. Has to be. These knees can't take many more trap doors."

"I like your knees!" BRO said.

"Don't be fresh," Mom snapped.

"Sorry!"

It was almost a surprise when *Moneymaker* took off from the Tower without proximity warnings or shield alerts. No one chasing them. No one firing on them. The surface was secure, or would be soon. With any luck, they'd make it to the Hold before Striker had the same thought.

When Hilda announced they'd reached orbit, Gareth left cargo and made his way to *Moneymaker*'s upper rear viewports. Where he found Sloane, standing with one hand on the window, her hair a mess of tangles from the wind at the top of the Tower. From above, Fane looked calm, its seas a splash of gem-toned turquoise against the growing expansion of black.

He wondered if the other people who lived on the planet had any idea of the battle that'd been raging at the Fleet Tower. Fane was the Fleet's home, but it *was* an entire planet. Full of cities and towns, communities, homes. Many of which he'd never even seen before. For a moment, it made him feel homesick, which made no sense; how could a person feel homesick for a place that had never truly felt like home? Or, stranger still, homesick for parts of it he'd never even seen?

Gareth hoped the CTF had spared the rest of the planet. It seemed likely; Striker's allies were quickly drying up. If the Fleet was stretched thin, the CTF must be stretched thinner. It had to be.

Then again, that was a thought that'd occurred to him before. And he'd been wrong.

"Striker knows the gateways aren't on Fane," Sloane said. "Isn't it possible he'd be *allowing* Alex to transmit messages to Ivy's inlays, leading us astray on purpose?"

"Possible, yes. Likely? I doubt it. According to West, Striker doesn't know any more than we do."

Sloane sighed. "The Hold is a wild guess. At best."

He looped an arm around her waist, and she leaned her head against his shoulder. "It's a good wild guess, though."

"I suppose." She tipped her head up to look at him. "But the gateways had better not be in that dinosaur-duck monster's nest. I'm not facing that thing again."

Gareth thought they'd be lucky if these supposed gateways were that easy to access. But he said nothing, merely watched as Fane grew steadily more distant.

"Incoming call!" BRO said. "It's President Simelda. He sounds like he's walking outside. I hear waves in the background."

"Thanks for setting the scene." Sloane straightened away from Gareth, a new crinkle deepening between her eyebrows. "Put him through."

"You're welcome!" BRO said.

Gareth could think of a few reasons why Simelda might contact them directly, and none of them meant good news. Unless someone had been exploring Lostelle's jungles and happened upon a bunch of ancient alien gateways. Unlikely.

Though maybe the president had heard back from Alisa March about joining up with their alliance. About abandoning Striker. That gave him cause to hope. Though surely Simelda would have contacted him about that personally, rather than pinging the ship.

"We've got a big slash of light in the sky above Lostelle." President Simelda might have been discussing the surf conditions or last night's beach party, his tone was so unconcerned. One of the President's well-practiced masks. He probably didn't even realize he was still wearing it. "I'm thinking it might be one of your wormholes."

Sloane let her head fall back, the crinkle deepening. "Striker found you."

"Looks that way."

It'd only been a matter of time. Still, Gareth had hoped there would be more of it.

"Question," Simelda said. Like he was inquiring about the weather forecast, or the outcome of the latest zeeball match. "In the event Striker aims his nightmare weapon at us. How do I know who to shoot at? What if he shows us clear skies and calm seas right up until enemy cannons come into range?"

"That's two questions!" BRO put in.

Before Gareth could think of how to reply, his mother's voice spoke up into the comms. Because obviously she'd given herself access to them. "I've got two operatives on Lostelle with immunity to the weapon," she said. "Jenkins and Cron."

Gareth wasn't sure why these revelations continued to surprise him. What would it be like to accept her offer? To direct operations on this level? When he'd taken command of the Fleet, he'd worried about living up to his father's excellent example. How could he hope to live up to his mother's?

With Sloane's help, he thought. He could do it with Sloane's help.

"How does she *do* that?" Sloane asked.

"They're headed toward you now," Candace added. Gareth caught a distinct note of smugness in her tone. Proud of herself, and her operatives. It was hard to believe she really wanted to give it all up.

"All right," Simelda said. "I'm standing on the beach at—"

"They know. Listen to them, do as they say, and we've got a chance of not killing each other with friendly fire."

"But really," Sloane said, "how do you do it, though?"

Gareth doubted his mother would give an honest answer to that question. Before he could confirm that, however, an eye-searing line of light split the space between *Moneymaker* and Fane. Closer than it'd been in the space above Aemlyn. And in atmosphere, too. He hadn't pictured the wormholes in atmosphere.

A wormhole in Lostelle. And now one in Cadence.

"Governor Wagner Penn is calling from Ve Station!" BRO announced. "He says there are four more wormholes opening in the Halorin System. And—oh! Now there's a message coming in from Elter! They have a wormhole, too. That's six wormholes. No, seven. Now it's eight. The other Cadence planets are calling in. You don't hear from them very much. Why do you think that is? Nine, ten—"

"Multiple wormholes," Sloane breathed. "All over the galaxy?"

"Eleven!" BRO said.

Doing his best to tune out BRO's tallying, Gareth squinted toward the silver-white line that had ruptured the space between Fane and *Moneymaker*. Just in time to see a pair of corvettes come cruising out of the wormhole, followed by a suite of cube ships.

Gareth opened a direct comm to Lager. "What are you seeing, Captain?"

"Big slice in the sky," Lager replied.

"Ships coming through?"

A pause. "Negative. Just open air, sir."

Gareth swore. "Get Sands on the bridge, trust his visuals. Make sure Pitorski's in charge on Fane and that they're firing."

"Yes, sir," Lager replied.

Gareth hesitated. "We'll need *Sabre* to hold them off while *Moneymaker* escapes to the Current. We have to get to the Hold." He didn't want to think about what a trip to the Current would be like, or shift the view screen to check the conditions there. It'd been rocky enough with one wormhole; now there were a dozen and counting.

"Sir, we were supposed to come with you."

Sloane was shaking her head. "If you don't cover us, those ships will stop us. There's too many of them."

Gareth looked at her. "You can see the ships?"

She nodded. "*Moneymaker* crew, sound off," she said. "Who can see the enemy ships out there?"

"I do, I do!" BRO said.

"I see them," Hilda confirmed. "Little assholes. And a few big ones."

Brighton, Ivy, and Vin confirmed. Even Escher left her lab to peek out of a viewport and do the same. Somehow, everyone on *Moneymaker* was immune to the hallucinations. What the hell were they missing here? None of them had been exposed to the stasis fields. Could it be something about smaller ships?

All questions they'd need to explore later. For now, they had to escape.

Mom appeared from the direction of the galley, helmet propped under her arm. "I see them." She pushed past Gareth, heading for the nearest pod. "I need to get to Zander's ship."

"Why, exactly?" Gareth asked.

She reached up to give him a pat on the cheek. "Because we need to spread out the brains."

"As long as you don't mean that literally," Sloane said.

"Hopefully not, dear. You find those gateways, I wager you'll win this war." She snapped her helmet on. "But do hurry. We haven't got forever."

And with that, she ducked into one of *Moneymaker*'s drop pods. A moment later, she was arcing away from the ship, heading for the *Starset*—which was also making for the Current. Off, hopefully, to help defend Lostelle.

"She didn't ask to borrow that pod," Sloane said.

"Probably because she doesn't expect to return it."

"Damian stole the other one," she complained. "We're out of pods."

A problem, but not the main one. Flashes of plasma fire arced out of *Sabre*'s cannons, taking out a pair of Striker's cube ships in a skid of liquid fire. They were too far away to see flashes of rail guns from Fane's surface, but Gareth hoped Farley and the others were deploying them. Or that they would soon.

"Take a seat everyone," Hilda said. "It's going to be a bumpy ride."

CHAPTER 17

BUMPY, Sloane thought, was a bit of an understatement.

Usually, a dive into the Current felt fairly seamless. It was a minuscule change, a shiver you'd hardly recognize if you weren't watching for it.

This time, it felt like the Current was swallowing *Moneymaker* whole. It jerked the ship, snatching it out of the Cadence System and blanketing them in gray murk. From the outside—and even from the inside, during their trip from Halorin to Cadence—it'd resembled smoke. Now, as she stood at the viewport beside Gareth, it looked like they'd plunged into the bottom layer of river silt to kick up clouds of centuries-old muck. If a flesh-eating river shark appeared outside the window, it'd fit right in.

Up close, the flow of the Current looked grainy. It looked *wrong*.

A thread of yellow light zigzagged out of the murk, and Gareth grabbed her arm a split second before it struck the ship. Which only sent them tumbling together as *Moneymaker* lurched in response, lights stuttering.

Sloane hit the floor hard, and she would have gone sliding

down the tilted hall if Gareth hadn't had the presence of mind—or pure luck—to grab the door frame that no longer led to a drop pod. She clutched his arm, legs flailing. She really didn't want to go sliding all the way through the galley to the pilot's deck. That would hurt.

"Ouch!" BRO yelled. "Static shock!"

"I think that was more than static," Sloane said as Gareth helped her climb up to grab the other side of the frame. The ship shuddered, then evened out. Sloane didn't let go of the frame, though. As soon as she could find a place to strap in, she would.

"That was fun," Hilda said through the comms. "Let's never do it again."

"We need to get out of the Current," Vin said. "It's too dangerous."

"And do what?" the pilot shot back. "We have to get to Adu. Unless we want to spend the next hundred years traveling there, this is our path."

Yeah, the Parse Galaxy was pretty much reliant on the Currents. As previously established.

"Good to hear you two getting along," she said.

"We're not," Vin and Hilda replied together.

Gareth let out a short laugh. "At least they agree on something." He had the sense not to say it through the comms.

Sloane thought they'd feel better if they'd just kiss already. Best not to say that, either.

For a breath, the comms were quiet. Sloane was just starting to wonder why that was when Gareth nudged her with his elbow. "Your call," he said.

Right. She was the captain. Sloane held onto the door frame, watching out the viewport as another sizzle of lightning skimmed past the ship. "Hilda's right," she said. "We keep going. We'll avoid the lightning as best we can. It didn't fry our systems, so hopefully we can handle another hit if it comes. Everyone had better strap in, though."

Even to her ears, it sounded like a terrible plan.

"Avoid the lightning," Hilda repeated. "Yeah, no problem."

"You're the ace. Brighton, get to engineering in case something breaks."

"On it."

Together, Sloane and Gareth made their way to the galley and slid into the booth. It was the closest spot on the ship that had straps—unless she counted the infirmary, but she didn't relish the thought of being stuck on a cot during a rough flight.

And it was rough. It was definitely rough. As soon as they were seated, the ship jerked to the side in a move that would have knocked Sloane to the floor again had she still been standing. For a second, the ship tilted so dramatically that her back was on the floor, and she was afraid her coffee beans would all come spilling out of the cabinet if the catches failed.

"It's not that easy to dodge lightning." Hilda sounded like she was pushing the words out from between her teeth.

"You're doing great," Sloane said. She wished she'd made it to the pilot's deck, though. She'd prefer to see what was happening instead of being stuck without any windows.

The ship swerved again, as if to reinforce the need to stay seated. Gareth braced his hands against the edge of the table as the gravity anchors once again pulled their feet toward the floor. *Sabre* could probably make a maneuver like this without disturbing a single soldier. He didn't seem to mind, though. Just gave her a little smile and a wink when he caught her eye.

At least they were together. And at least Cadence was right next to the Bone System. Sloane didn't think she'd be able to take more than a few hours of getting jerked left and right. And occasionally even hit, despite Hilda's best efforts. Every time the lights stuttered, she wondered if they'd lose life support this time. If the Current would rip the ship apart.

As it was, Sloane felt like her teeth had been rattling in her head for a year by the time *Moneymaker* began its approach to the Bone System. At which point she and Gareth risked leaving their seats to join Hilda and Vin on the pilot's deck. Sloane actually wasn't clear on why Hilda was allowing Vin to sit with her, but he did immediately vacate the co-pilot's seat when Sloane arrived. She accepted it, but mostly as a matter of principle—her ship, her chair—rather than because she cared all that much.

The gesture gained him half a point in the forgive-Vin game. His vigil at Hilda's bedside had earned him three. No, five. At this rate, he could expect to be back in Sloane's good graces sometime in the next year or so.

Hilda's good graces might take a little longer to restore.

Sloane didn't think she'd ever been so glad to leave the Current. She braced herself as Hilda made the exit, prepared for the river to snatch them back in, but it let the ship go without a fight. And Sloane took her first deep breath in hours.

The Current wound unusually close to the outer objects in the Bone System, which always made the exit a bit startling. Which she could say with a certain amount of authority now, because of the many, many times she'd now visited this place. Maybe more than any System in the galaxy besides Elter. One minute they were surrounded by a swirling river of smoke, the next they were sidling up alongside an outer asteroid. Close enough to wave hello, and to see the pattern of pockmarks on its surface.

It wasn't out of the realm of possibility that the Currents had originated here. They'd been mapped, but Sloane wondered if anyone had tried to figure out where the map began in the first place. Likely so. There were probably dueling groups of scientists duking it out about their various ideas on the subject.

Sloane didn't know why she was so certain they'd find these gateway things at the Hold. Maybe it was her lingering dinosaur-duck phobia—a phobia based on real trauma, thank you—or the memory of the criminal cartels who'd taken up residence there and forced Gareth and Damian to fight to the death.

Or maybe it was just what made sense. The Bone System's defeated dictator might be long gone—well, not *that* long gone; gone enough—but the Hold had been his key stronghold.

If he really had been some of kind of alien, using alien tech that was advanced enough to feel an awful lot like magic... then yeah, he'd probably been keeping the road back to his own part of the galaxy close.

Sloane didn't want to dive into Sever's twisted thought processes. Unnervingly enough, it was what she'd have done. Which was why they'd asked the copper bot and its companions to start their hunting scans here and work out toward the rest of the System if necessary.

It wasn't much more than a hunch. But she thought it was a solid one.

"Last time I was here, there was a lot of traffic going in," Gareth said, derailing her train of thought. Probably a good thing. It'd been on its way to running off course.

"The last time you were here, Callow Clan and the Mechics were running a colosseum show with you and Damian as the main attractions," Sloane replied.

"Good point. Though I wasn't technically an attraction until I went down to save Damian."

"And promptly got yourself caught."

"Details."

Vin shifted in his chair, plainly uncomfortable at the exchange—he might accept that Gareth was a good guy, but he was obviously still reconciling himself with the idea of them as a couple—but Hilda just rolled her eyes. "I'm ready to go back to my coma now."

"The copper bot says they have a possible location on the gateways!" BRO said.

Sloane frowned, tapping her fingertips on her knee. They'd sent the bots on ahead, but still, that was fast. Much faster than she'd have anticipated. "Why only a *possible* location?"

They were hunter bots. Usually, they pinpointed their quarry down to the meter. Often less.

"CB says, 'there is an untamed mist through which the truth is no more than a conjecture.' What does 'untamed' mean? Will the mist try to bite me?"

Sloane blinked, trying to sort through the wall of words to interpret an actual report. She supposed she could see Dad's point about the bots. A little bit.

Gareth cleared his throat. "Maybe you can ask the copper bot for clarification."

"I hope so! I'm confused!" A pause. "CB says there's something blocking the signal. It also says that artistry is wasted on the masses."

That actually sounded somewhat promising. If the gateways were easy to find, they'd have been discovered by now. Especially with all the cartels that'd been picking this System apart since Sever's disappearance. "Is the copper bot okay with you calling it CB?" she asked.

"I will ask." A pause. "Yes! It says nicknames are an indication of brotherly camaraderie."

Hilda raised a hand and snapped her fingers. "Sloane. Focus."

Right. "Have I mentioned I missed you, Hilda?" Sloane asked.

"Nope, and I've been crying on the inside. BRO, send the coordinates. I'll bring us down."

CHAPTER 18

MONEYMAKER TOUCHED down in an open area near the coordinates the bots had indicated. As the gangplank lowered, Sloane had to shield her eyes against the glare of the place. Brighton headed out first, with the copper bot on his heels, and she followed slowly, fumbling in her pockets for her sunglasses. Didn't need those much in space.

Gareth was a step behind her, with Ivy taking up the rear. She'd never been much of a talker, Ivy, but she'd been nearly silent over the last couple of days, and the pinched expression around her eyes suggested she hadn't been sleeping well.

They'd get Alex back. They had to. Sloane kept thinking that if they found these gateway things before Striker did, they'd be able to set a trap for him. Ambush him for once, instead of the other way around.

If Sloane had to describe the landscape, possibly for a school paper or a travel guide, she might have said that the place looked as if some mythical king had come down and touched the ground, turning everything into sandstone and then polishing it to a glossy shine that made her eyes ache even through the sunglasses.

Everything here had that reddish-brown tint to it, from the ground to the towering rock formation that loomed ahead.

It was like standing in a big, dustless desert. She might have thought it was natural, except for the strange flatness of the ground, like all the curves and bumps had been sanded away and slapped with a coat of varnish.

And when she tilted her head back to study the formation, she couldn't help but notice the unnatural bluntness of the walls —they were as flat as the ground beneath her feet—and the sharp points of the corners. Not a naturally occurring structure, though it gave the impression of trying to blend in. She'd have said that the boxy formation was blocking her path, except for the sinking sensation in her gut that told her that the formation *was* her path.

"Please tell me we're nowhere near the flying colosseum," she said.

Gareth was studying the formation as if he, too, thought it might hold their destination. "Other side of the planet."

Brighton, who stood several paces ahead of them with his rifle at the ready, said, "Does this count as a planet?"

Sloane glanced around. The last time she'd visited the Hold, her stay had been mercifully brief. In fact, one might even argue that she'd never been here at all, since she'd only touched ground in a flying colosseum. To rescue Gareth and Damian from certain annihilation via dinosaur-duck.

"It's roundish, and it's got its own atmosphere," she said. "It's not a station."

"Is that where the line is?" Brighton asked. "Round, with atmosphere? What if the atmosphere's artificially maintained? Does that make it a station, even if the surface is natural?"

Sloane shrugged. Scientists could make all the distinctions they wanted. If it looked like a planet and let her breathe like a planet, then she'd be calling it a planet. Unless it was *orbiting* a planet, in which case it'd be a moon. No need to overcomplicate the issue.

Besides, she suspected Brighton was chattering more from nerves than because he actually thought she'd come up with an answer.

And she couldn't blame him. The surface of the Hold felt strange and overly cultivated, and it smelled sterile. No hint of greenery, no birds winging overhead or lizards scrambling for cover under overly glossy rocks. When she took a step, her boot touched down on clean, grit-free rock, and the sound disappeared quickly into the open sky.

No breeze. No water. Nothing but rock.

"Okay," Sloane said. "Let's follow that signal. Lead the way, CB."

Sloane didn't understand how it worked, when she'd given the bots an image of the gateways rather than an energy signature or something useful like that. But the bots hadn't flinched at it, and they seemed confident enough that their target was somewhere in this area.

There was nothing to do but follow the coordinates. Sloane started toward the rock formation, casting a wary glance at the sky. The formation cast no shadow, but she couldn't see Adu's light directly above, either. The light seemed to come from everywhere at once. Not disconcerting. Not disconcerting at all.

"Anyone else starting to wonder if we're walking in a simulation?" she asked. They'd only been walking for a few minutes, yet they'd almost reached the wall. She hadn't seen it move closer. Had she?

She had to work hard to keep from slowing her steps, from delaying the mission. She pushed herself forward instead, ignoring the instincts that were screaming at her to run as fast as she could in the other direction.

Brighton moved along with her, quickening his steps to lead

by a few paces whenever she happened to step ahead of him. It was impressive how seriously he took his job. She'd definitely write a stellar recommendation letter if he ever wanted to apply elsewhere. Though hopefully he wouldn't.

"Seems solid enough," Gareth replied.

CB had rolled to a stop outside of the rock formation, as if awaiting further instruction. "The signal is straight ahead," it said.

Sloane stepped up beside the bot, blinking away the this-is-weird feeling of the too-even lighting. And then she reached for the wall.

"Maybe don't do that," Brighton said.

She didn't expect anything other than the obvious: that her fingers would brush against the weirdly smooth, sandstone-like stuff. She definitely didn't expect her fingers to melt straight *through* it.

Only that was what happened. She touched the wall, and it... yielded. It wasn't a hologram, like Candace's trap-door-hiding trick on Fane. The surface felt cool, not quite liquid but not quite solid, either. So Sloane did the only reasonable thing she could think to do; she kept pushing, ignoring Brighton's cry of protest as she stepped straight through the wall and into the rock formation.

She didn't want to contemplate how hefty those therapy bills were going to be at the end of all this.

Brighton rushed straight through the wall to join her, followed by Gareth and then Ivy. CB came last, as if it had the most sense out of any of them. Gareth merely lifted his eyebrows at her, like 'Really?'

Brighton, though, had *his* eyebrows tucked together in a disapproving glare. "You couldn't have waited for us to check it out before diving right in?"

"Have you even met her?" Ivy murmured.

Exactly. He was just mad she hadn't let him go first. "It's just an illusion," Sloane said. "I'm sure I can turn around and step right back through."

To demonstrate, she turned and placed her hand on the wall. Which she could do, because the wall was solid. Not that liquidy, almost-solid feeling, but *solid* solid.

Sloane pushed her palm flat against the too-smooth stone. It didn't budge.

Brighton sighed, and Ivy gave him an I-told-you-so shrug. But Gareth said, "We need to go this way, anyway. Safety is beside the point."

When he put it that way, it sounded pretty dire. Not that he was wrong. If the storm in the Currents told her anything, it was that Alex's universe-implosion warnings were less of a theory and more of a definite outcome.

The gateways might be able to shut off Striker's wormholes. Or at least stabilize them somehow. That was the whole point, right?

As soon as they saved the universe, they could focus on the galaxy. Best to take it one huge, humanity-level threat at a time.

With the exit sealed, Sloane turned back around to face the road ahead. Except that there wasn't one. Not exactly. They were standing in the center of a wide passage that stretched to the left and right, with another sandstone wall blocking the direct path ahead. The ceiling, if there was one, soared too high to make out. The eerie everywhere-light continued, which was even weirder in here than it had been when she'd stood on the surface.

Brighton leaned forward and gave the wall in front of them a tap. "Solid stone."

"So we can turn left, or we can turn right," Sloane said. "Anyone got a coin we can flip?"

"Or," Ivy said, "I can scan for nearby tech and try to bring us through the most direct way."

"Or that," Sloane said.

Ivy's inlays pulsed, and a line of silver-blue light scattered down the wall like a wave. Ivy's eyes went wide, and she stumbled, grabbing her head with one hand. Sloane caught her elbow before she could fall. After a moment, the inlays went dark.

"Feedback." Ivy forced the words out between gasps of pain. "I can't."

Sloane held Ivy's arm for another moment, until the other woman righted herself with a nod of thanks. "I say we go left," she said.

"Why?" Brighton asked.

Sloane shrugged. "Feels friendlier."

Gareth drew his pistol, nodding at the security officer. "Let's go."

Not that long ago, he'd have wanted evidence. Facts. In truth, the whole place felt equally unfriendly. But they had to pick a direction. Fifty-fifty chances here.

CB led the way, its wheels rumbling along the stone passage. The only other sounds were the strangely muted footsteps, and the occasional hush of their clothing brushing against the walls. Sloane wouldn't have been all that surprised to find that the passage was magically long, far outpacing the length of the rock formation they'd seen outside. Or that it was set up like a carnival funhouse, with mirrors to confuse them.

But the rock-walled corridor merely led them to a nondescript corner. No signs praising them for choosing the right path. No trap door. No riddles. No booby traps. They rounded it with weapons drawn, Brighton and Gareth heading in right behind the copper bot.

"How great would it be if we just found the gateways now?" Sloane muttered.

No one answered, not even to offer a quip about how unlikely that was. And on the other side of the wall, the passage forked again.

Sloane groaned. "I was always terrible at mazes. I got in trouble for drawing straight through the walls."

"Of course you did," Gareth said.

Before she could think of a good comeback, the wall in front of them broke apart.

Sloane staggered back, afraid of a rockslide. But instead of crumbling, the rocks rose up, defying gravity to reorganize themselves into a huge and plainly humanoid shape. It shifted, the rocks scraping and scattering bits of dust and gravel as the monster reared back, preparing to strike them with its huge, reddish-brown fist.

Okay, so there was a trap here, after all.

Sloane didn't wait to see if the monster could be reasoned with. She ran, listening for the others' footsteps behind her, but not daring to look back. The ground shuddered as the monster's fist came down, sending tremors vibrating through the stone.

She threw herself around the next corner, sensing the others close behind, but there was no way a thing that size wouldn't catch up with them. Two steps, and it'd be there. Maybe three.

A shot blasted toward her from up ahead, and she threw herself to the ground by instinct before realizing that sliding along the passage on her belly would slow her down. By a lot.

Would she rather get crushed by a monster, or blasted in the face? What a choice.

But the shot arced above her, blazing up to crack into the monster's rocky chest. Whoever the shooter was, they were aiming at the monster, not at Sloane. Her frantic brain threw out theories of long-lost space pirates stuck in the maze for all eternity. With her face pressed to the sandstone, she couldn't begin to guess who was really doing the shooting.

"Stay down!" Sloane didn't recognize the voice that called the warning, either, but she didn't care. She stayed down, glancing back in time to see Gareth and the others following suit.

A second blast hit the rock monster in the head, and she glanced over her shoulder in time to see it stagger backwards, flailing for the wall. She wouldn't have expected a rock-headed monster to be felled by any blast—did it have a brain in there?—but the shot must have pinpointed whatever tech was running the thing, because it crashed into the wall and shattered, stones grinding and falling apart as it fell, landing in a pile of rubble.

Breathing hard, dust clogging into her throat, Sloane scanned for her friends. Gareth was right by her, Brighton and Ivy behind him. The copper bot had paused at her side, as if it didn't quite understand the delay. Or maybe it was writing an epic poem about the monster's demise. Who could say?

Sloane pushed to her feet, ready to thank the rock-monster-blasters for their assistance. When she lifted her head, though, the words died on her tongue.

Striker was thinner than he'd been the last time they'd run into each other. And he'd already been on the rangy side. His vest was unbuttoned, forehead smeared with dirt, and his shocked expression said he had no idea whose life he'd just been saving. When a pair of CTF-banded soldiers came rocketing around a corner from the other direction—the maze was already making her dizzy—she put it together. Striker had thought he was helping his own team.

"Surprise," Sloane said, almost choking on rock-monster dust. "Where's Alex?"

Striker stared at her for a beat, eyes flicking to where Gareth and Brighton had their guns trained on him. Calculating his chances.

He must have calculated against himself. Because instead of firing on her, he turned and ran, his soldiers falling in at his sides.

Gareth moved to fire, but Sloane said, "Don't shoot. Look."

In the center of Striker's group, a shock of red hair stood out.

"Alex!" Ivy cried, but the group was already gone, disappeared into the obscurity of the maze.

Sloane pulled her shooter, glancing back again to make sure the monster was truly gone. "Come on," she said. "This just turned into a race."

CHAPTER 19

GARETH HAD to agree with Sloane; mazes were overrated. It was beyond frustrating to see the coordinates of the bots' readings in the scanners without being able to reach them directly.

But they couldn't draw over the walls—or climb them, or break them—and it wouldn't do them any good to wish otherwise. If Sever had been the one to place the gateways here, he'd certainly done it with a dramatic flair.

"Why isn't Striker using his hallucination-maker to change the way the maze looks?" Sloane was still clutching her shooter—a bit more casually than he'd have suggested—but they hadn't run across any challenges in the last ten minutes or so.

"Maybe he is using it, but they don't work on any of us," Gareth said. Striker had no way of knowing that anyone was immune. "Maybe they simply don't work in here."

He couldn't imagine Adu's dictator allowing a weapon like that to function within his maze. He would want the control over every twist and turn. Any added illusions would ruin the drama of these sweeping walls, the polished floors.

But judging by the way those walls had flickered in sympathy with Ivy's inlays—not to mention the appearance of a potentially robotic rock monster—they were more than they appeared to be.

"Maybe he didn't expect to need them," Sloane said. "Maybe he threw us off course on purpose. Sent us to Cadence as a delay."

Certainly a possibility. Striker breathed manipulation.

"We don't even know what this hallucination weapon looks like," Brighton said. "Maybe they need a ship's cannon to make them work. Maybe it doesn't even fit in here."

"Does anyone else smell mangoes?" Sloane asked.

Brighton frowned at her, like he was annoyed that she'd ignored his theory, then paused, tipping his chin up. "Actually, yes."

There was a definite sweetness in the air that hadn't been there a few minutes ago. Mangoes and cherries, Gareth thought, though there was definitely something sharper in the mix, too. Something acidic.

They rounded another corner to find that the copper bot had paused before a thick curtain of vines. The leaves were as thick as coins, the edges soft and bordered in splashes of milky white. When Gareth traced the vine's path back up toward the ceiling, he could see that the web crisscrossed back and forth between the walls, too tangled to let him locate the source. Nearer the ground, though, the vines evened out into a hanging curtain. It looked like they should be able to push the vines aside and simply walk through.

Yet even Sloane hesitated, stopping just shy of touching them with her fingertips. "Anyone know what these are?"

Gareth shook his head. Brighton bit his lip like he didn't want to find out, while Ivy tilted her head, examining the leaves as if she might have seen them before but couldn't quite place them.

"I miss Alex," Sloane said. "She'd be like, 'I'm an astrophysicist, not a botanist!' And then she'd tell us exactly what they are and why we should stay far, far away."

"She's here," Gareth said. "We'll get her."

"She's on the other side of the vines." With a final grimace, Sloane stepped forward, using her elbows to shove the vines gently aside. Gareth followed, and the air immediately turned heavier, the strangely ubiquitous light of this place shifting to a greenish tint as if someone had placed a filter over the source. There was no way to tell how far the passage stretched.

"This isn't so bad," Sloane said, pushing another vine aside and picking up her pace.

"Don't say that," Brighton groaned. "Never say that."

The copper bot trundled along beside Sloane, letting the vines trail over its hat-like plate. "An oasis on the cusp of danger," it sang.

One of the vines twisted suddenly, grabbing for Sloane's ankle and yanking her into a stumble. She caught herself against the wall, then jerked back with a cry of pain, her palm blushing an angry red. "It stung me," she said. "The *wall* stung me."

"Not an oasis," CB sighed. "Pity."

Gareth peered at the wall. It was shinier here, somehow. It looked almost wet. "The plants must secrete that stuff." Could the vine have pulled her toward it intentionally? Surely plants didn't have *intentions*... "But why—"

A rustle spattered through the leaves, and Gareth shoved Sloane forward as nettles rained down on them from the matted vines above. The nettles struck his armor and fell away, but when one landed on his neck, its stingers pressed into his skin and held on, pushing into his flesh and sending thrills of pain down his spine.

Gareth raised his armored hand and pulled it out, drawing blood. Given the chance, he was fairly certain it would have drilled all the way in. "Carnivorous vines."

Or were they parasitic? At this point, he wasn't sure the distinction mattered.

"I think they like to hunt," Ivy said.

There wasn't time to consider what *that* meant, as a fresh shower of nettles broke loose to patter down toward their heads. Sloane was already running, head ducked, hands raised to protect her head and neck from the worst of the onslaught. The nettles stuck to her hands, and she pulled them off as she ran. They caught in the strands of her hair that weren't tucked into the armor, and she brushed them away with her sleeve.

Vines struck at Gareth's feet, attempting to knock him into the wall—or so it felt—but he yanked his boot free, throwing his weight forward to avoid falling sideways. Brighton was cursing and Ivy was breathing hard, but at least he could hear them. At least he knew they were still there.

As for CB, the bot made it through the mess of vines without any trouble. As if the plants knew not to bother with metal and bolts. Not digestible, apparently.

The rest of them dashed through the leaves, twisting and tripping and dripping blood onto leaves that absorbed each drop with eager thirst, turning the milk-white borders red. For a breath, or maybe two, Gareth thought the passage might go on forever. That eventually, the vines would manage to catch them, to pull them against the stinging walls and devour them in a cloud of stinging nettles.

And then they were out, the vines dropping away as suddenly as they'd appeared, the passage opening back into reddish-brown walls and colorless light.

Gareth used his gloved hands to brush the last few nettles out of his hair, checking the collar of his armor to make sure none had sneaked through. Ivy and Brighton were doing the same.

"Everyone okay?" Gareth asked.

Sloane nodded. Her ungloved hands were covered in

bleeding sores, and he stepped forward to pluck a stray nettle out of her hair as Ivy pulled the first aid kit out of her pack.

"At least someone thinks of these things," Sloane said, holding out her hands so Ivy could wrap them in bandages. "Those little jerks better not've been poisonous."

A concern that hadn't occurred to him. "All the more reason to hurry."

"Ahead," CB said, "our destination beckons."

Sloane, who'd been watching Ivy's progress with the bandages, looked up. Gareth did the same, peering down the passage to where several more tunnels joined them from either side. From the looks of it, they could have taken any road to reach this central corridor.

Not that those roads were likely to have been easier than theirs. Because when the passage opened, it spilled out into a wide plaza. A plaza that was surrounded by pearlescent doorways.

"The stabilizers," Gareth said. "We made it." Striker was nowhere in sight, and Gareth found himself hoping the man had run into trouble with some of these vines. He wouldn't regret that, as long as Alex made it through.

Sloane blinked at the plaza, like she needed to convince herself she wasn't looking at one of Striker's tricks. "Let's go."

Gareth followed a step behind, pistol ready. As far as he could tell, the passage was clear. And maybe Brighton's anxiety was starting to get to him, but that worried him.

They'd made it halfway down the corridor when a shadow rushed out of one of the side passages, giving Gareth just enough time to register its presence before ramming straight into him, knocking him shoulder-first into the ground. He gripped his pistol, twisting to aim it at his attacker. Not one of Sever's tricks, but a CTF guard. The man landed on top of him with a grunt, an angry red wound on each cheek, a dribble of blood leaking down along his hairline.

Sloane turned back, and Gareth caught sight of a missed nettle in her hair as she paused, obviously divided on whether to help him or run for the gateways. But Gareth could see shadows hurrying toward them through the passage. Striker and the others, right on their heels.

He'd be fine. "Go," he said, struggling to flip the CTF guard onto his back. The man flailed, aiming a blow to his jaw and snapping his head to the side.

Sloane hesitated for a final beat. And then she ran.

CHAPTER 20

SLOANE HAD to trust Brighton to help Gareth. She ran, Ivy on her heels, CB rolling along beside them like this was just a pleasant stroll through the park. She could have sworn she heard it humming.

It would have been good to come up with a game plan, but it was difficult to strategize when you were in the middle of a psycho alien's maze and trying to reach one of the most important pieces of technology ever unearthed in the history of the galaxy. Before a wannabe emperor and his dogs could get to it first.

And that wasn't even an exaggeration.

A shot skittered off the stone to her left, and instinct pushed her to the right, slamming her shoulder into the opposite wall and slowing her down. Striker wasn't aiming at some rock monster this time, that was for sure.

She pushed forward, begging her body to move faster, to stay upright, to use her forward momentum to run instead of fall. She didn't know what she'd do when she reached the gateways. She only knew she needed to reach them first. Take the higher ground, the defensive stance.

Another shot glanced off the floor. Was Striker aiming at

her feet? Seriously? She danced away from the shots, well aware of how quickly a bullet to the heel would finish this little mission.

Blood pounded in her head, the nettle-tastic pain in her hands pulsing to the same beat as she drove herself forward.

There might be one way to reach the gateways more quickly.

"CB," she said, "lift me up."

The copper bot surged forward like it'd been waiting on the command, snatching hold of her belt as it took off in a rumble of wheels and clacking claws. Her feet left the ground with satisfying speed. Definitely faster.

And definitely the wrong call. A hundred percent the wrong call. Because the minute they went airborne, Striker got a clear shot. Bullets pinged off the copper bot's rollers, and it gasped in protest as the impact pushed it into an uneasy zigzag, muttering something about heinous murderers.

"Keep moving," Sloane said. "We have to get there first."

"Alas, that flight should leave me," CB moaned. "I am damaged. I am killed. I cannot take to the skies, and I mourn that I will soon plummet."

"We're all of ten feet off the ground," Sloane said. "I think you'll be fine."

Not that she was excited to fall ten feet. Could definitely mean a fracture or two, but she'd live.

"The flesh yields. The metal cracks. Such is the way of the—"

"Then drop me," Sloane interrupted. Dad was right about this one. Totally off in its circuits.

And unfortunately, CB took the order literally. Which, yes, she'd intended for it to do, only with a bit more warning. So it was still jarring when it released her right above the doorways.

She caught herself on the frame by the armpits, her shoulders taking the brunt of the hit as she landed, clicking her teeth forcibly together. She'd thought she might be able to land on top of the frame, maybe walk it like a balance beam. Now, though, it was clear that they were much too thin for that.

Ivy probably could've managed it, graceful as she was. Sloane was lucky to be hanging here at all.

Striker stood in the center of the gateways with Alex. He'd made it to the winner's circle, but he looked wild, unhinged, as he draped one arm across Alex's collarbone, holding her in front of him like a shield. Her red hair was flying in every direction as she struggled.

At least, until Striker lifted his pistol and pressed it to her temple. Then she went still, eyes wide with fear.

If there was one thing Striker's defensive posture told her? It was that he was alone. Or he thought he was. Sloane twisted to catch a glimpse over her shoulder, which confirmed that Gareth had dispatched his guard. The man lay sprawled out in the passage, and she didn't know if he was dead or stunned. Either way, he was out of the race.

There were no others. Had the maze taken them out? Or had they abandoned their boss? She hoped it was the latter; might gain them some more allies. Not that they could be trusted, but there was an extent to which a gun was a gun, as long as it was pointed at a mutual enemy.

"Now what?" Sloane asked Striker. She was still hanging above him, but too far to jump down and kick him in the face. So much for the high ground.

"I'll kill her," Striker said. "She's the only one who can make a wormhole, and I'll kill her."

Sloane's eyes drifted to the gateway behind him, where a distinct icon had been carved out of the white material. The outline of a knife. She'd have thought it a decoration, if she hadn't encountered that very blade before. In another galaxy. In another world. Probably couldn't get through to those friends now, though.

She wasn't sure they'd help her, even if she managed it.

Sloane kicked, trying to work out the best way to stall. "See, again," Sloane said, "you're telling us why *you* don't want to kill her. Leading with the wrong thing. Here, I'll help you. She's our friend. That's why *we* don't want you to kill her."

Striker actually looked confused, like he couldn't fathom choosing friendship over wormholes.

While he was trying to work that out, the frame behind him blinked. And then the pearl-white doorway blinked on, as if someone had pressed a switch that read GLOW NOW. The arch filled with wormhole-like ripples, sending a blast of blue and white light splashing across the plaza.

Maybe she'd accidentally summoned her Milky Way friends, after all.

When the gateway spit out a person, though, Sloane released the door frame in surprise, falling to the ground in a heap of abused limbs.

The person who stepped through the doorway? It was Damian.

CHAPTER 21

THE LAST TIME Gareth had seen Damian Riddle, the man had been disappearing into the Current in one of *Moneymaker*'s pods. Running away.

Now, his friend strode out of the stabilized wormhole like he'd just stepped out for a quick errand. His hair was wild, like he'd left another fight to join this one, and his long duster jacket flapped around his knees. Gareth would have sworn the man had left that coat on *Moneymaker* when he'd stepped into that airlock to martyr himself, but there was no questioning its presence now.

Damian had brought his own bots with him, though they weren't like CB and the others. The first was a small, rodent-shaped machine that sat on his shoulder, its tail swishing like a warning. The second was tall, its head triangular, its limbs long and spindly. It stalked in after Damian, and something about the forward-leaning hunch of its posture suggested that it might be sulking.

And that was all the time Gareth had to absorb the scene before Damian was fighting, taking full advantage of the element of surprise to rush Striker from behind and knock Alex out of his arms. She stumbled forward, but Ivy rushed forward to catch her, helping her up and hurrying her quickly away from the fight.

Striker whipped around to return Damian's blows, but the tall bot intercepted him, throwing its rod-like limbs up to shield Damian from attack. Striker's hits landed on the bot's arms, and he staggered back, bending double and clutching his own arms against his body as he yelled out in pain.

Gareth headed for Striker, ready to cuff him and drag him off to justice. In his mind, he could already see the man's would-be empire crumbling without its figurehead. Striker would go to trial. The CTF would be disbanded. And order would be restored.

Too easy. It was always too easy.

Three CTF guards leapt onto the plaza, joining the fight from three directions and shattering Gareth's hopes that they'd been lost to the maze. He turned away from Striker and Damian to block the closest one from interfering in Striker's fight. He caught sight of Brighton in his peripheral vision as the big man met the second of the guards, and of Sloane somersaulting to avoid the third.

And then Gareth was lost in his own hand-to-hand. Close quarters to take a shot, even a stun round, and any one he tried might go wide and hit one of his friends.

His CTF opponent had no such concerns. He'd come running at the battle with his gun drawn, a fat-barreled monster of a weapon that looked like an aspiring mad scientist's pet project. Gareth hadn't seen its like, but he knew he didn't want to give the guy a chance to pull the trigger.

He threw himself at the guard from the side, slamming his stunner into the guy's gun-holding wrist. The man grunted, wheeling around to aim a blow at Gareth's head with his other hand. Gareth ducked, taking the opportunity to hit the man's center of gravity with two punches to the stomach. Why Striker hadn't dressed his guys in armor was anyone's guess.

Unfortunately, the guard had managed to keep a hold on his weapon despite the hit to his wrist. It might've been fused to his fingers, he held it so tightly. He attempted to raise it, but he'd have done better to try to shoot Gareth's feet; they were too close.

Gareth knocked into the guard's shoulder, trying to maneuver a heel behind the guy's knees and drop him to the ground. But his opponent's footing was solid. Even on the defensive, he kept Gareth from moving close enough to fell him.

And then a metallic flash scurried across the plaza to swirl around their feet, like a manic cat at feeding time. The guard's heel caught on the squirrel-like bot, and he tripped, his gun-holding-hand swinging wide as he fell. Gareth slammed his elbow into the barrel of the gun, finally knocking it out of the man's hand. It slid across the plaza, stopping at Damian's feet.

Damian ignored it, still intent on his battle with Striker, but the squirrel-sized bot skittered forward to bat it out of the way. It looked like a pet rodent trying to play with a toy meant for the family Rottweiler.

It did the job, though. The gun skidded out of Striker's reach, and the CTF leader's momentary distraction allowed Damian to land a solid kick to the man's stomach. Striker doubled over, coughing, but before Gareth could step in to arrest him, the last-standing guard appeared at his boss' side. And he was brandishing a hand cannon.

But Brighton had one, too, and Damian bent casually to scoop up the stumpy weapon the bot had dragged his way. If the CTF guard took a shot at one of them, the other would take him down. But neither could their group make a move on Striker without forcing him to pull the trigger.

A standoff. Not the best.

Striker staggered, clearly trying to recover from the blow to his stomach. "I don't need gateways to lock the galaxy in a hallucination." His voice was little more than a rasping choke. "Not when I've got the Currents."

He backed away from the plaza, his final loyal guard covering their retreat.

"Shouldn't tell us your plan," Sloane mumbled. But she was on her back, wiping blood away from her mouth, and she kept squeezing her eyes shut and opening them again like she was trying to right her vision.

Alex and Ivy were kissing and crying, holding each other tightly. If nothing else, they had Alex back. That was worth everything.

"I'm sorry I almost imploded the universe again," Alex said.

"Join the club." Damian extended a hand to Sloane, helping her to her feet before turning to Gareth. He had a cut on his forehead, another on his neck. Gareth didn't know if they'd come from this fight, or another one.

As soon as Sloane was on her feet, she threw her arms around Damian. His eyes widened in confusion as he let her hug him, staring at Gareth over her shoulder like he needed an explanation. Gareth just shrugged. "Sometimes, your family chooses you," he said. "Like it or not."

When Sloane stepped out of the hug, she stared at Damian for a long moment. And then she slapped him across the face.

"What the hell was that?" she said. "Where the hell have you been? We thought you were dead."

She punctuated the last word with a smack to Damian's shoulder.

Damian touched his hand to his cheek. "I think you may be right, Commander," he said. "This does feel like family."

CHAPTER 22

SLOANE COULD THINK of more pleasant places to camp than the center of the creepy, gateway-surrounded plaza on the deposed dictator's home planet. Like literally anywhere else in the galaxy. She'd prefer a muddy Fringe planet over this place, where evil vines had tried to eat them and the feeling of unseen eyes trickled along her spine like a constant threat.

The passing hours hadn't dimmed the strange everywhere-light. She'd traveled enough to know you couldn't rely on the light to tell a story of passing hours—every planet was different, in that respect—but it was still a strange feeling. It left her feeling off kilter.

The gateways were blinking, too, their pale frames lit with parades of tiny lights. Ever since Damian's arrival, they'd been flickering like that. Like they wanted to welcome him. If they were smart, they'd warn him away instead.

It might not be the best place to rest, with hard polished floors and alien gateways, but she couldn't deny the necessity. They lacked the resources to guard the gates and chase Striker at the same time, so they had to wait for *Sabre* to bring reinforcements.

And after that sojourn through the maze, there was no doubt that they needed rest. Still. She didn't have to like it.

Damian leaned against one of the gateways, legs stretched out long in front of him. His lip was bleeding, and he had cuts on his forehead and neck, but he grinned at her when she came over to sit next to him. It had to hurt, but he didn't show it.

"Not afraid to touch the gateways?" she asked. Everyone else in the group was sticking to the middle of the plaza, as if they wanted to stay as far from the alien technology as they possibly could. Every instinct in Sloane's body said she ought to be doing the same.

"They like me." Damian nodded toward the bot with the triangular head, which had taken up a standing position beside him, still as a statue. Not interested in sitting, apparently. "This is Bruce. And the rodent is Triv, at least for the moment."

The rodent bot was sitting on his shoulder, where it'd returned after the fight. Sloane supposed that if Damian was going to have a familiar, this one fit his personality. "I don't understand why a bot should be shaped like a squirrel," Sloane said. "What good does that do?"

"No idea," Triv said. "It's repulsive, isn't it?"

Sloane blinked at it, confused. A self-hating bot? Though actually, when she thought about it, that tracked pretty well with the others she knew. "How long have you known these bots?"

Damian fluttered his fingers at her. "I'm too tired to think of an evasion, so you'll have to imagine one for yourself. I'm sure it'll be almost as good as mine would've been."

Infuriating as ever. "Do you do it out of spite?"

He looked thoughtful. "Out of habit, I think."

"Well," she said, "I'm still glad you're back. And not just because you saved the day."

The tall bot—Bruce—made a sound that might have been a

sniff. "He is not back," it said. "He is running a test. One that *ought* to have ended several hours ago, I might add."

It said this last bit with a pointed tilt of its head in Damian's direction. Damian merely propped his hands behind his head and settled back against the gateway. Like it was a lounge chair instead of coveted alien technology. "No rush, B," he said.

The squirrel bot pinched him on the ear, and he winced. "All right, they've got a point. I do have to go back. I didn't expect to run into you. Ever, if I'm being honest. And definitely not at this precise moment."

Sloane looked over her shoulder at Gareth, who was sitting near the center of the plaza and not bothering to hide the fact that he was listening to their conversation. He just gave his head a small shake, as if he had no idea. She wondered if he'd met these bots before, since he and Damian were such chums. Surely if he'd known where Damian had disappeared to, where he might be going, he'd have said so.

"I'm hesitant to ask this," Sloane said, "but back to *where*?"

Bruce let out a whirring sound. "You do *not* want to know."

She actually really did. She ignored Bruce, keeping her gaze on Damian. After a moment, he sat up, wincing again, and touched a finger to his swelling lip. "Did you have to hit me?"

"Yes. And the lip wasn't even me. Stop being dramatic."

"I suppose that's fair." He might still be infuriating, but he also seemed... tired. Worried. Sloane watched him, trying to think of something she might be able to say that would get him to tell them the truth.

Before she could come up with something, he shifted. "I'm sick," he said finally.

"That, we knew," Sloane said, not bothering to hide her impatience. Ivy and Alex had been trying to help him, right up until the moment he abandoned them to throw himself into the Current.

"Well, the answer's there. Through the gateway. Maybe a cure, maybe not. But I have to find out."

Where, though? Sloane wondered. Where did the gateway lead? To the people—beings—who'd created the gateway technology?

It must be.

"Can we come with you?" she asked. "Would they be willing to help us?"

"I wouldn't recommend that," Damian said.

"But you're willing to go back."

"Again. Sick. Dying. Want to not die." He blinked, hard.

"Also," Bruce said, "there is a very cranky reporter waiting for him. Her features are what you would call 'in line with the aesthetic standards of beauty that one would expect to attract a man of Damian's cultural upbringing.'"

Sloane didn't think she would ever in her life call it that, but she got the gist. Damian had a girl. Interesting. She raised her eyebrows. "Oh, really?

"It's not like that," Damian said.

"It is," Bruce said, "exactly like that. He simply does not know it yet."

Damian shot the bot a glare. "Shut up, Bruce."

Sloane decided to trust the bot's word over Damian's. "In that case, I hope you'll bring her for dinner next time you're in the neighborhood."

"She wouldn't... you know what, never mind." Damian got to his feet, moving like his limbs felt heavy. He crossed the plaza to speak with Ivy, and Sloane turned away to give him at least the semblance of privacy with his sister. Not the easiest thing, in this open space, but she did her best.

The squirrel bot—sometimes Triv, whatever that meant—skittered down from Damian's back, hopping across the plaza to run a circle around Sloane's feet. And then it leapt up onto *her* arm. Its paws tickled where they pressed into her sleeve.

She almost shook it away. Instinct.

"By the way," Triv said, "the bot that's accompanying you is operated by a deceased human's consciousness."

Sloane blinked. "I'm sorry, what?"

"So is the one it's communicating with," Triv continued, as if she hadn't spoken. "On your ship."

"The Currents as well," Bruce put in. "It is all rather flummoxing. But I have confirmed the facts."

Sloane opened her mouth, then closed it again. "Human consciousness," she repeated.

"*Deceased* human consciousness," Triv corrected.

Damian returned to their side of the plaza, shook Gareth's hand, then moved over to stand in front of the gateway. It flared to life

"Wait," Sloane said, stepping toward the gateway. "You need to explain."

"No time," Damian said. "Murderous reporters. Very scary."

"Human consciousness?" Gareth said. "That's the answer?"

"Deceased human consciousness." Triv seemed pretty hung up on the deceased thing, like it was a crucial distinction.

Damian looked back over his shoulder. "It's true," he said, extending a hand toward Triv. The small bot launched itself from Sloane's arm to land on Damian's outstretched one, and then Damian was stepping back through the gateway with Bruce a step behind.

As soon as they were gone, the lights blinked out.

"He might have told us how to use the gateways," Ivy said. She sounded like there were tears in her voice. Poor Ivy. She'd just gotten her girlfriend back, only to lose her brother again.

Sloane turned to face the group, their stunned expressions mirroring her thoughts. It was almost comical, the way they all stood there with moon-wide eyes, lips parted, staring at the empty space behind her where Damian had disappeared.

"Okay," Sloane said. "What did we learn?"

That the galaxy was much bigger and much more confusing than they'd originally thought it was, for one thing.

"I think, therefore I am more than a box of wires and bolts," CB said. "What a relief."

A relief. And an explanation, too. BRO and the junk-pile bots—it sounded like a particularly terrible band name—had all originated in this other sector of the galaxy. Their quirks weren't just artificial intelligence trying to figure out what it was. They were *human* intelligence.

"BRO and the bots, our bots, are run by the same tech as the Currents," Sloane said. "Human consciousness, somehow. Also, Damian has a girlfriend."

"Focus," Alex said. Like she was one to talk.

"So they're human," Gareth said, "and they're also alien. Human aliens."

Sloane shrugged. "We've met human aliens before, in the Milky Way. If it happened twice, it could've happened three times."

Or there was more to the story, and they'd all originated in the same spot somehow. But that was a question for another day. Maybe a question for the age. Though she had a feeling the wormhole stabilizers would open up whole new areas of study, assuming they could figure out how to use them. And protect the damn things from Striker. It seemed more likely now, yes, but he'd made it abundantly clear that he wasn't finished.

They hadn't won. Not yet.

"If the bots are run by the same technology as the Currents," Gareth said, "it could explain why Zander's ship wasn't affected by the hallucination weapon."

"Dad had bots on board," Sloane said slowly. "They somehow countered the effects."

"And BRO did the same when we were leaving Cadence," Brighton said.

It explained why Gareth heard whispers in the Currents, and in the stasis fields. It explained everything.

Of course, it also created about fifty million more questions. Another problem for later. The 'later' file was getting thicker by the second.

"We need to get a bot on every ship we've got, as soon as possible." Sloane headed for the plaza exit, wishing there was time for a brief nap. "We can't wait for *Sabre* to get here. Brighton, Ivy, you hold the plaza with CB. Alex, you're coming back to *Moneymaker* with Gareth and me. We need to get to Striker."

CHAPTER 23

GARETH STARED out of *Moneymaker*'s viewport as the Current drew nearer. It was becoming a favorite spot; from here, he could see Striker's needle-thin ship making a run for the Current, a tiny streak that he wouldn't have been able to identify without help from the overlay screens.

The little ship was fast. But *Moneymaker* was fast, too. And they had to catch up.

Cadence and Lostelle had confirmed that with Alex's return, Striker's network of wormholes had vanished from their skies. Gareth could see for himself that the lightning storm in the Current had faded, and that it was back to its usual turquoise flow. No imploded universe today. Or at least, no imploded Currents.

And the whispers were real. If the tech was run by human consciousness, it explained everything, from the bots' eccentricities to the differences in the stasis fields' reactions to his presence. Some had been hostile, some kind, some desperate. They *were* different voices.

Maybe they were trying to be reunited. Trying to be one.

"I knew I was human!" BRO said, and not for the first time. "I knew there was a reason I fit this crew! You're human! And I'm human!"

Kind of, Gareth thought. But there was no need to rain on the AI's joy. Though he supposed he'd have to stop thinking of BRO as an AI at all.

He tried to imagine a world where all the technology was run by these voices, these consciousnesses. BRO and the others hadn't been aware of what they were before today. That much was clear. Had the knowledge been programmed out of them? How had they arrived here in the first place—and why wasn't this other section of the galaxy communicating with them?

So many questions. Damian knew the answers, but he was gone. Gareth didn't know if his friend would ever return.

He pressed a hand to the window, grounding himself against the cool material. At least the fight with Striker would be finished soon enough. Sloane was already fussing with her pack on the floor behind him, though he was pretty sure she was moving things around more than adding new ones or inventorying them. She checked her shooter's charge for the third time, then sat back to lean against the wall. She'd be antsy until she could take action, a feeling he understood well enough.

If *Moneymaker* intercepted Striker's ship, they'd disable it, then board and arrest him.

If Striker hit the Current ahead of them, the mission would get ten times more complicated. Gareth had a feeling that was the mission Sloane was preparing herself for. The worst-case scenario.

He could picture her directing a room full of operatives, sending them off on various assignments before leaping onto *Moneymaker* to handle the most dangerous one herself. He could see the partnerships she'd form, the digging she'd do. The dangerous corners and secret dealings she would unearth. He could see how she'd fit into his mother's world.

Strangely enough, he could also see how he might fit into it.

"Striker gave something away back there." Sloane clenched her fingers into fists, released them, clenched them again. Restless. "He used a stolen Interplanetary Dwellers book to find the gateways, and Damian used a stolen Interplanetary Dwellers book to reroute the Currents. Striker must have found a way to use the Currents to flow the hallucinations through the galaxy."

Gareth had to assume it was a less efficient way than the wormholes, or at least more complicated. Especially as the resistance kept taking out his allies.

"We can't get bots to everyone," Sloane continued. "We have to stop him before he starts convincing them to murder each other."

"Or turn on us," Gareth agreed. It wouldn't matter if every ship they commanded came with one of the bots; if Striker managed to convince every person in the galaxy that they were the real enemies, then the citizens might well rise up. Take over surface rail guns and commandeer grounded ships to shoot their own protectors out of the sky before they knew better.

No matter how many broadcasts they put out, no matter how many messages and assurances, there would be chaos.

Even if they could deliver bots to every household in the galaxy, GRO was the only one able to travel the Currents on its own. They'd never distribute them in time. Which meant they were racing the clock. Not his favorite thing, especially when they had no way of knowing how much time was actually on the damn thing.

All the more reason to catch up with Striker, and quickly.

And in the background, the Current called to him. They were almost there, and the voices were already murmuring in the background, like the babble of a brook just around the bend.

Almost intelligible. Beckoning. Were they friendly voices? Or would they rip him apart? He suppressed a shiver.

"Striker's running out of allies," Sloane was saying. "He didn't have an army down there. He had four guys. He's got the better weapon, but he's running scared. Desperate."

It might be true. Or it might be wishful thinking.

As the thought crossed his mind, three ships exited the Current in front of them. Not the hoped-for backup from the Fleet, either. The viewport stuttered in alarm as it rushed to alert them that the weapons were hot, the lasers painting *Moneymaker* with targets.

The three ships were followed by three more, and three more, until he couldn't count them any longer.

"Who's *that*?" Sloane asked.

Gareth's words stuck in his throat. He knew the sleek, feather-thin design of these ships—as beautiful as they were deadly. He'd flown on them plenty of times. He cleared his throat, swallowing back a wad of panic. "They're Alisa's," he said. "They're Torrent Trio ships."

Sloane swore, clambering to her feet. "Still on Striker's side. How dense *is* she?"

He didn't feel himself capable of answering that question.

Gareth's direct comm chimed, and President Simelda's name scrolled across his eye screen. Gareth nearly laughed. A little late for an update on how his conversation had gone.

But then, Alisa would've planned that. She would have used Gareth's hope of reconciliation to her advantage. Gareth accepted the call.

"She's standing firm, Commander," Simelda said. "And I think she may be headed your way."

No kidding, Gareth thought. The outcome of their discussion was all too clear. "Understood," he said as Striker's ship zipped straight through the line of Torrent ships, like a minnow seeking the protection of a school of whales.

"We can't get to him," Gareth said.

Sloane clenched her fists, expression narrowed in concentration. "Yes, we fucking can," she said. "BRO, get Horace Brennan on the comms. Now."

CHAPTER 24

EVEN IN HOLOGRAM, the derision on Horace's face was plain. The thickset man had twisted his lips into the expression, as if she'd said, 'derision? what's that?' and he wanted to give her a demonstration. Eyes narrowed, nostrils flared. Somewhere between condescending and very, very angry.

Still upset about that card game of his, probably. Boohoo. She was upset about the damned fate of the galaxy.

When Horace's eyes flickered to Gareth, Sloane could almost see the obscene insult as it formed on his lips, his anger giving way to a smirk.

But Sloane wasn't going to give him a chance to speak. She started talking first.

"You see those pretty lights pouring out of the Current, Horace?" she asked. "Even your pathetic scanners should be able to pick them up. Go ahead. Wave to your little cronies. Tell them to get working on it. Those are Torrent Trio ships. Here in the Bone System."

Horace's mouth was still open, still ready to spew some ill-thought-out insult at her.

"Alisa March would like nothing better than to put every

surface out here under her jurisdiction," Sloane continued. "You know what that'll mean. Rules. Checkpoints. Cops. All of it. The end of your business, at the very least. You in handcuffs, or buried in dirt. Trials and jail time, and whole hidden cities rooted out of their hiding places. It'll be the end of your freedom in the Bone System. Can you see it, Horace? Can you imagine it?"

Horace closed his mouth. Sloane decided to take that as a 'yes.'

She lifted a finger, jabbing it toward his image. "Get the hell out here and defend your system," she said. "I'm sending two dozen bots your way. Distribute them, one on each ship. They'll protect your people against mass hallucinations. Otherwise, you'll be standing there thinking your copilot's your lover, and it'll get really ugly really fast when he decides you're *his* enemy. You won't want to see where he jams the nav stick."

Horace's eyes widened. "Mass hallucinations?!"

It was the first thing he'd managed to choke out. Good. "Hallucinations," she confirmed. "Get. Over. Here."

"I—"

"And by the way," Sloane added, "I don't work for the Fleet. They work for me."

She ended the call. If she relaxed her fists, her hands would be trembling uncontrollably. She wasn't sure if that was out of nerves or anger. A combination of both, most likely.

She wouldn't know if her little play had worked until it worked. Or until Alisa's ships turned them all into slag.

Seemed like a long shot.

When she glanced at Gareth, he was staring at her, gray eyes unreadable. For a second, he looked like the same distant, unapproachable Commander he'd been the first time she'd met him. And the second time, and the third time. Back straight. Hair too damned neat for a person who'd been stumbling around mazes and fighting CTF goons.

"What?" she asked. "Too reckless? Too rude? Be nice to the criminals, they hold our lives in their hands? Or could at least get us some cheap electronics?"

He shook his head. And then he grinned. In spite of all the danger they were in, it sent sparks through her stomach. "Actually, it was excellent."

Sloane let out a breath. Not that she needed his approval. But then, she did value his opinion. To a point. "Thanks. Do you think it'll work?"

"It'd work on me."

"That's the problem, Fortune. It has to work on criminals, not on goody-goody Fleet Commanders."

He looped an arm around her waist, pulling her close. "Haven't you heard, though? I'm a traitor now. On the run."

"Any chance you could talk to your friend Alisa and convince her that's not the case?" she asked. "Beg for your life one more time?"

"I can try." He bent to kiss her. "Better do it from the guns, though."

If her hands would stop shaking long enough to trust them on the controls, sure. "I'll take the second one," she said. "Maybe she'll remember she loves you, and we won't need to shoot at anything."

As she wedged herself into the gun tower, she couldn't help feeling like the chances of that were pretty slim. It was hard to believe that Alisa March would have stayed by Striker's side merely because she thought Gareth was guilty of murdering the FAC. If true, that would have been bad—Sloane had never denied it—but Alisa was a leader. A politician. Surely she could see the bigger picture.

Luckily, Sloane had taught Gareth everything she knew. If he hadn't absorbed her silver-tongued ways by now, he had only himself to blame.

CHAPTER 25

IN THE MERE seconds it took for Gareth to get from the viewport to the gun tower, Alisa's ships had opened rows upon rows of hangar bays. The doors yawned, maw-like, as they spit rows of fighters out into the vacuum. It was like watching a leaf split in half. Hard not to remember those carnivorous vines on the Hold, and the way they'd dropped their nettles.

As he watched, the fighters zoomed toward *Moneymaker*, each one opening fire as soon as it came within range. The shields absorbed the shots easily, for now—he couldn't even feel the shots, though some of them had to be landing—and Gareth hesitated, hands on the gun controls. What was Alisa's play here? Keep her big ships at a distance to protect the fighters?

Or keep her ships at a distance so that she wouldn't have to do more than stall?

"We're starting to take fire," Hilda said over the comms.

"What, those sparks?" Sloane's voice replied. "That's nothing."

"Unless they wear down our shields so the big guys can take us out."

"Point taken. Try to evade. Gareth? Are you going to make a call, or...?"

Gareth opened a comm to Alisa. He couldn't help feeling like it was what she wanted him to do. She wouldn't make the first move; he had to come crawling. He didn't like the feeling.

When she answered, her voice was harsher than he'd ever heard it. "Give yourself up, Gareth."

She certainly didn't waste any time.

"Not the friendliest greeting, Alisa," he said.

"Cut the crap, Gareth. You know pleasantries make my skin crawl. Turn yourself in and face justice for your crimes."

Pleasantries made her skin crawl. Sure. He'd spent entire weeks at her estate that'd been lathered in pleasantries. Woodland walks, meadows, horses. Cornbread. She'd acted the hostess, to the point where it'd been difficult to imagine her as a politician at all, even after he'd become the Fleet Commander. Now, he couldn't help wondering if that'd been the point.

Had his father seen through it? Gareth certainly never had. And they'd kept returning there, year after year. So either Dad had seen a political reason of his own to do so, or he'd seen Alisa as a friend.

He was glad his father wasn't here to witness what that 'friendship' had truly meant to her.

True friend or not, Alisa was too savvy to believe that Gareth could be responsible for the massacre on Cappel. Maybe she'd been shocked into believing so at first. But she couldn't have accepted it for long. It was impossible.

She was waiting for his response.

"This isn't about me anymore," he said slowly. "It hasn't been, for a while. If it ever was?"

She was quiet.

"You don't believe I murdered those people," he pushed. "You support Striker. Admit it."

"And why shouldn't I?" she hissed. He'd put her on the defensive; that was good. "He's right. He's always been right. There's another inhabited part of the galaxy, one that somehow bestowed the best of our technology onto us. One of these days, those gateways will open and spill armies into our midst. Our best hope of beating them is a united front."

"And an empire is the way to do that?" Gareth kept his own tone measured, trying for a counter to Alisa's anger. Her desperation. Whatever future Striker had painted to get her on his side, it must have been a terrifying one. But his sympathy only stretched so far.

"It's one way," Alisa replied. "And if we have to bend everyone's brains to accomplish it, then we will. They'll thank us for it."

So much for sympathy. "I doubt that."

"Then you won't be there to see it. You're outgunned, Gareth. I don't want to shoot down your little freighter, but I will. I think we both know it can't hold up to an onslaught from my fleet."

Gareth gripped the gun controls, wondering what good it would do to fire at the fighters. Or at Alisa's ship, for that matter, if he could bring himself to do it. Not that *Moneymaker*'s cannons had much hope of taking out the massive Torrent Trio vessel. It'd be a questionable undertaking even without the swarm of fighters zipping around between them.

Moneymaker was still taking fire from the fighters, and he was glad he was strapped into the gun tower as Hilda evaded with her usual skill, swerving to avoid the thickest sections of fire. Good to have her back; Gareth doubted Vin could fly so well. He certainly couldn't.

"How long have you known?" he asked. "That I didn't murder those people?"

Alisa hesitated. He'd surprised her, he thought. "A... for a while, Gareth. But I *did* believe it, for a time."

Then she was exactly the fool he thought she was. No; she was worse. And she was awfully defensive for someone who truly believed herself to be in the right. "And when you learned otherwise?"

A longer pause this time. "It was necessary," she said finally. "A new galactic order. The cost was—"

Gareth shut off the comms, disgusted. Whatever else she had to say, he didn't want to hear it. Nothing could justify the murder of innocent people. Nothing.

"Good try," Sloane said. "Though maybe you should've kept her talking a bit longer."

Gareth refocused in time to see the sea of fighters part, like someone had carved a path straight toward them. Making way for the largest ship to barrel toward them: Torrent's flagship, bearing Alisa's green standard. She was on it, in the thick of the battle.

There wasn't much to respect about her anymore. But at least he could respect that part. She'd come to fight in person.

Of course, it *was* easier to enter a battle when you had the biggest ship. "How close is *Sabre*?" he asked.

"Still hours out," Vin replied. "We're on our own."

Alisa's guns flashed, and Gareth braced as Hilda jerked *Moneymaker* out of the way. Though the fire was everywhere, even with Hilda's skill, he didn't see how it could be avoided for long. The ship shuddered as the shields absorbed the blow, but the searing yellow streaks said Alisa wasn't letting up. A ship like that had enough firepower to shoot at them for days. If they retreated deeper into Adu System, she'd overtake them quickly. And the closer they got to any inhabited surface, the more innocent people would be in danger.

"Shields at thirty percent," BRO said. "As a newly minted human, I wish to say that I'm afraid to die."

"You're still not a human," Sloane said. "Not exactly."

"Rude!" BRO said.

The ship shuddered.

"Shields at twenty-two percent," BRO said. "It has been an honor. A privilege. A—"

"Shut up," Sloane said. "We're not dead til we're dead."

"But our shields are at twelve percent," BRO said. "That looks like dead to me."

Gareth hated to admit it, but that pretty much looked like dead to him, too. Alisa's barrage kept coming. She didn't care if she killed him; she'd absorbed Striker's zeal. And no one was coming to save them. The Current sang in his ears, offering a thread of hope. So close—it was *so* close—but still too far to reach. Alisa's fleet was blocking them in.

Gareth swallowed. "Sloane—"

"Not you, too," she said. "I don't want to hear it."

"Five percent," BRO said. "The next hit—"

A star bloomed in front of the Current as Alisa's ship exploded, piercing through the black with sharp beams of light. Like a child's drawing of a star. The thought drifted up through his shock as the fire burned, hot and bright, then contracted, *Moneymaker*'s systems alerting them to the heat, the new threat of incoming shrapnel.

Hilda pushed *Moneymaker* back and away, swerving to avoid what she could before the battered shields failed. It would be a shame if they'd survived this long only to die by shrapnel to the hull.

Gareth's throat was dry, and he couldn't wrench his eyes away from the wreck. Alisa had made her choices, but he was still sorry for it.

"I'm afraid to ask who just took out that ship," Vin said.

As if in answer, a pair of Fox Clan dragon ships swooped in from either side, sending several of the remaining fighters up in sparking balls of flame. Like miniature replays of their flagship's destruction.

This time, the dragon ships weren't their enemies. They were an escort.

"This is our System," Sloane's criminal friend said, his voice gruff and resigned through the comms. "We've got your back. Run."

CHAPTER 26

SOME PART of Sloane's brain thought that she'd died. There wasn't any other explanation for the fact that the Bone System criminals had actually come through to help her. She had to be dead, assigned to some purgatory where she'd be forced to relive her final battle over and over.

Or maybe it was a happy afterlife, where she could live a version of the battle where she actually won. Though that'd be a weird afterlife. She'd have expected more chocolate, somehow.

But Hilda was whooping through the comms, and Vin was, too. They were still here. They still had voices. Though maybe they were dead, too. Sloane pinched her own leg, hard, then winced. Death probably didn't come with nerve endings.

"Horace," she said, opening a comm to her new best friend in the entire universe. "You made it."

Dragon ships as escorts. She never thought she'd see that day. And when she told her scope to show her a three-sixty view, she could see an entire mismatched fleet behind them, dragon ships floating majestically alongside spindly mechic ships and freighters that looked like they'd been cobbled together with duct tape and spit. They all had guns, though. Even the duct-taped ones.

The criminal clans. Working together. Not just in a card game or a cash-cow colosseum show, but against the actual bad guys.

Horace grunted. "Your bots are weird," he said. "One of them wants a pickle. I haven't *got* a pickle. It said it'll take a rain check."

Huh. She hadn't met that one. Bots didn't eat, so she wasn't sure what that was about. Maybe it just wanted to smell it. Or 'take in its atmospheric readings,' as BRO would say. "They're helpful, though," she said. "Keep it up. You took out the flagship, but there're still fighters out there."

Horace grunted again. "No 'thank you'?"

She grinned, releasing the gun controls and giving the seat a spin. "We're going to save the galaxy. It's the least you could do."

Also, they'd taken their sweet time about it. But she didn't need to insult their capabilities. They *had* shown up. It was something. A leader should be encouraging, right? Firm, but encouraging. She could do that.

Horace cleared his throat. "You know," he said, "Fox Clan could always use a mind like—"

"No, thanks," she interrupted. "Now, we still have to cut through the battle to get to the Current. Make sure you don't let the rest of those fighters shake up my *Moneymaker*."

Silence. Except for Hilda, who cleared her throat.

"It's a Milky Way joke," Sloane said. "Shake your *Moneymaker*."

"What's a Milky Way?" Horace asked. There was a cautious note in his tone, like he was afraid she might turn on him if he offended her. Or like he thought she'd lost a few marbles in that battle.

Joke was on him. She'd never had those marbles to begin with. Sloane sighed. "Never mind."

"If it helps," Hilda said, "I understand the joke, and it's still not funny."

Sloane wedged herself out of the gun tower. "I said never *mind*."

Gareth was already waiting by the viewport when she stepped out of the tower. She hadn't even gotten to shoot very much this time. Always a bummer.

"We did it," she said. "They listened to me."

Gareth was clearly trying to look happy, but she knew his real smile, and this wasn't it. She felt her own grin stall on her face as she tried to read the worry behind his. "What is it?"

He glanced out at the nearing Current. It was unblocked now, nothing in the way but the spinning wreck of Alisa's ship and a few lonely fighters. It was a relief to see its swirling blue again, instead of that freaky smoke monster it'd been before.

"I need to communicate directly with the Current," he said.

That was one way to get her attention. She stared at him. "I'm sorry, why exactly?"

He stepped closer, finally looking away from the Current to meet her eyes. "Capturing Striker is one way to stop this. But we've got to attack this one from two sides." He drew in a deep breath. "I can shut off the weapon. Convince the Currents not to carry it."

Sloane pursed her lips. She didn't like it. "That sounds iffy."

"But possible," he argued. "You have to admit it is. The tech literally has a mind of its own."

"And we have no idea what's motivating that mind." She wanted to grab his shoulders and shake him. "That mind might be on board with Striker's plan. It might be on board to annihilate our part of the galaxy. You don't know."

"I don't. But I have to try. You go ahead and stop Striker. I'll hit the Current directly." He paused. "I'll meet it, that is."

Yeah, wouldn't want it to feel threatened. Sloane lifted her hands to his upper arms, gripping him tightly. If she insisted that he abandon this plan, he might do it. But part of her whispered that he was right. If Plan Stop Striker failed, they needed another way to cut off his weapon.

"Fine," she said. "But nothing good ever comes from us splitting up. I'm not going to let you pull a Damian. We're in this to work together, not break apart. Otherwise, I don't see the point of winning."

"Saving the galaxy, for one," he said.

He was trying to make a joke, but it was a bad one. "That's just it," she said. "I don't think we can even do that unless we stick together. The Current wants to talk to you? It can damn well talk to you from right by my side."

Gareth looked at her for a long moment, then pulled her into a hug. "I didn't understand your Milky Way joke, either," he said. "But if I had, I'm sure I would have laughed."

She sighed into his shoulder. "I know. Maybe one day I'll take you there."

"I think I'd like that."

Sloane opened a comm to Hilda. "Take us into the Current."

CHAPTER 27

FROM THE OUTSIDE, the Current looked perfectly normal, flowing along in its usual snakelike formation as if it'd always maintained its blue-green tint, as if no one had tried to drain it of its stasis fields or implode the universe by opening a dozen wormholes at once. Gareth could help but admire its resilience.

And yet. As the Current absorbed the *Moneymaker*, images flooded across the viewport, some of them flickering too fast for his brain to compute. Sections of Obsidian City's skyline, a stretch of farmland. A System from the distance—he thought it might be Ilya—and a lonely street with thunderheads gathering in the sky. They passed like thoughts, grains of sands caught in a tide. Here and then gone.

Some remained, however. Some were solid.

But impossible. They were *impossible*. Traveling through the Current wasn't like traveling through normal space, true enough, but it was still *space*. The Fleet Tower couldn't float by, for example, looking real enough to startle him into touching the glass.

Gareth pushed his shock aside, reaching for calm. It was time to assess what he could see, not insist that it was impossible. Once he did, it was easy to make out the translucence that bordered even the most solid images, the way they blurred into the waves of Current. And then the Tower flickered away, ghostlike, to be replaced by the interior halls of its tech vault. He recognized a version of the transmissions Alex had sent to Ivy. Like they were on replay, reverberating through the entire Current, perhaps with the rest of Striker's thoughts as a backdrop.

Gareth swallowed. "Can you see that?"

She nodded. "The hallucinations."

Even with BRO to protect against them, and even with Gareth's repeated dips into the immunity-granting stasis field, Striker's hallucinations were thick here. They looked like ghosts, at least, impressions of reality. The longer he studied them, the flatter they appeared. Too flat to be read.

"Sloane," Hilda said. "I think you'd better come see this."

It was probably too much to hope that she was referring to the images. They made their way to the pilot's deck, where Vin was seated in the copilot's chair. He started to rise as they entered, but Sloane waved him back down, perching on the edge of the jump seat behind him and peering out of Hilda's viewport. They could have gotten this same view from the back, but there was something about seeing it head-on that made it seem more real, somehow.

At first, Gareth didn't understand exactly what he was seeing. Only that someone, presumably Striker, had erected a platform in the center of the Current. And was using it to ride through the flow. The platform didn't share the same frayed edges as the hallucinations, instead sharpening as Hilda maneuvered closer. It was real, then.

It didn't look Current worthy, in the least. Like Striker had bolted a twisted, tube-like apparatus onto a huge square plate and then tossed it into the flow. Where had it *come* from?

"What'd he do, flatten out his cube ship?" Sloane asked.

"They're not supposed to do that," Gareth said.

"I'll let it know the Commander said so." She was studying the setup with narrowed eyes, and when she leaned over to the dash to increase the zoom, it was clear that in addition to the machine, there was a figure standing on the platform. From here, it looked like he was surfing through the Current, barely maintaining his hold on the platform even though he had to be wearing magnetic boots. There was no way grav anchors would provide the pull he needed to stay on that thing.

Though to Gareth's knowledge, no one had ever *tried* that. The only thing he knew for sure was that Striker was exposed to the full storm of the Current. He was flailing around out there with what looked like useless motions, the tubes bucking wildly around him, but as the images shifted—Fleet Tower fading into a vision of huge, snakelike spaceship—Gareth suspected he was merely working the technology that created the pictures.

"Striker," Sloane said. "He's desperate."

And he was alone. Sloane looked at Gareth. "Can you shut off the hallucinations?"

"I can try." He hesitated. The song was there, but it was muted. Was Striker doing that? "I still think I need to get closer."

Sloane sighed. "I was afraid you'd say that. Get your gear, Commander. We're going out."

"That's insane," Vin said.

"And yet, we've done it before. Hilda, can you keep pace with the platform?"

"Nothing to it." Hilda said it through gritted teeth. "Don't get killed out there, Captain."

Sloane squeezed the pilot's shoulder, then turned to face Gareth. "Come on, Current whisperer. Let's go end this."

No pilot but Hilda could have matched pace with Striker's platform-station, and even she had to leave a gap too long for a tether, which left Gareth and Sloane to rocket into the tide without a backup plan.

At least they were tethered together. But Gareth couldn't shake the idea that it wouldn't last. It couldn't.

The moment the airlock twisted open, the Current's song flowed into Gareth's mind. Like the hull was a pair of earplugs that's been muting the song. Whether that was Striker's doing, or something else, he didn't know.

Sloane stepped out of the airlock, and then they were rocketing toward the platform. Gareth let her lead, focusing on letting the song wash over him. He needed to let it in; he needed to speak to it, the way he'd spoken to the stasis fields. But how did one speak to the Currents? The stasis fields already spoke. They whispered. Even if their words could be difficult to identify, their feelings usually weren't. And they understood him.

How did one interrupt a song to make a request? How could he add his voice to that chorus? He didn't know the harmonies.

Just one more question he ought to have asked Damian.

The Current accepted them more readily this time than it had the last. It still felt like competing winds were ripping at his suit, but he thought they might be tugging him toward the platform rather than raging against him. It felt like they wanted to talk to him, but didn't know how. Common ground, perhaps. But how to increase it?

The platform loomed closer, giving Gareth a moment to consider whether Striker truly had dismantled his cube ship to make it possible. Though it looked big enough, wide enough, to have been made from several cube ships. They were cobbled together, as if welded. How Striker had managed that, Gareth didn't know.

Sloane grabbed hold of the edge of the platform, hooking her tether to the grated surface, and reached for his hand.

When his feet hit the platform, the Current's song vanished.

It wasn't muted, like it had been on *Moneymaker*, and it wasn't distant. It was *gone*. His throat went dry, but he'd known it, hadn't he? He'd known it would happen.

Perhaps that was why it *was* happening.

Sloane was already moving, and she paused, turning back to check his progress. The look on his face must have given him away, because she said, "What's wrong?"

"I can't hear the Current anymore," he said. "I can't follow you."

"You have to follow me."

He bent and released his tether from where it tied them together, then hooked it to the edge of the platform beside hers. He could only hope the Current wouldn't demand that he release it.

Though he decided not to share that concern with Sloane. If he did, she'd never agree. "This time," he said, "working together means splitting up."

"Ugh," she said. "Fine. But if you're not here when I get back, I'm going to kill you."

He raised a hand to indicate his understanding. And with one last look at her face, he leapt off the edge of the platform and into the heart of the Current's song.

CHAPTER 28

STRIKER HAD A KNACK—A talent, really—for finding truly awful spots to work in. Honestly, the man was a prodigy, and here he was, wasting his talents to take over the galaxy when he could've been working for a carnival, creating the best House of Terror ever seen. What a waste.

The open-Current platform was as difficult to cross as Sloane had expected it to be, the Current clawing at her atmo suit from every direction, her knees suggesting not so subtly that perhaps she ought to let the magnetic boots go and simply float to where Striker was running the show in the middle of the platform.

She could see his outline, arms wheeling above his head, but he was mostly obscured by a curtain of flickering images. They made him seem much farther away than he actually was. The pictures spooled out and away from him like he was some kind of mad scrapbooker, Fleet Tower hallways bumping up against the Obsidian City skyline, cube ships dipping toward her fast enough to make her want to duck even though she knew they weren't real.

The last thing she needed was a look inside this man's head.

Ignoring the creaking protest from her knees, Sloane kept one boot at a time firmly locked to the platform. She didn't want to trust her hold on the platform to a single tether line, no matter how strong it was.

And she definitely didn't want to think about what that meant for Gareth, who was tethered *to* the platform and trailing behind it.

With every step she took, the images thickened.

"You really are desperate," she muttered. He had to be. All his enemies were cornered, outnumbered. He was out here alone.

But as soon as the thought crossed her mind, the curtain of images shimmered and shifted, materializing into a jumble of ships arranged outside of Lostelle's atmosphere. The bubble-like picture bumped up against similar views above Fane, Elter, and Aemlyn.

Enemy ships poured out of the Currents, streaming toward the planets in numbers she couldn't imagine were real. In the visions, they met with no resistance, easily passing Fleet ships and planetary defenses.

"Confusion," Striker said. Into her comms, or through the Currents, she wasn't sure. Anger burned behind each word, lending a hiss to his voice that was all too appropriate. "Everyone's too afraid to shoot at anyone else, in case the enemies they see are really their friends. All the work you did to bring everyone together. All for nothing."

Sloane could hardly make out the regular flow of the Current now. The images were too thick.

And she didn't believe them. She couldn't. Her people's ships had bots, and they had officers whose exposure to the stasis field in the bands rendered them immune. They knew who to shoot at, who to take down. And for once, they actually trusted each other. She had to believe they were trusting each other.

Which made this just another lie.

Sloane stepped forward, pushing through the curtain of

images, so thick that it slowed her like it was made of gel. She wondered, fleetingly, if it would trap her the way the rock formation on the Hold had. "You're going to break the Currents if you don't stop this," she said.

When Striker's face appeared among the images, his lips were twisted into an impossible sneer. She couldn't tell if it was the man himself, or another illusion. That could be a problem.

"I'm going to *save* us," he said.

But Sloane was barely listening. She let her eyes skip above the vision, above the pictures that swirled like threatening ghosts to where she could still make out the uninterrupted turquoise tides that surrounded the platform.

Break the Currents. That was how they could stop this. They had to break the Currents.

Gareth, she sent through her eye screen, *shut off the Currents.*

A pause, and her heart hammered fearfully in her chest as she tried to decide whether the hesitation was because of the request or because he was lost to the Current, his tether snapped. Would the Currents deliver him back to her, or steal him away?

Then, Gareth's voice in her ear. "I'm sorry, what?"

Sloane let out a breath that sounded much too loud in her ears. "Trust me."

"I do," he said.

The moment stretched, while the images in the Current thickened and thickened, the story of Striker's lies piling on top of one another. They weren't just meant for her; they were meant for the entire galaxy. A story to fool the individual fighters still skirmishing in Ilya, Halorin, Torrent. *Your battle might be won,* the images said, *but everyone else's is lost.*

The winners in Cadence would think everyone else had lost. The winners in Ikor and Erbor would think the same, and on and on until Striker managed to stall, to pick up the pieces and hammer them with a final blow.

Would those who could see the illusions trust those who saw reality? Or would they give in to despair?

"Come on, Fortune," Sloane whispered.

The moment stretched, taffy-long.

And then the Currents went dark, taking the images with them, and the platform dropped into the depths of interstellar space.

CHAPTER 29

STILL. Everything was so still.

Sloane stood on Striker's platform, mere steps away from the man himself. The images had made him seem far away. Unreachable. But he was right there. If she'd pushed through them, taken another two steps, she'd have been there.

But the stillness made it easier. Off to the left, *Moneymaker* kept pace with the platform, making it appear frozen against the backdrop of stars. She probably should've thought to warn Hilda about the shift. Maybe Gareth had.

She didn't turn to see if Gareth was still with them. She didn't ask if the Currents were off throughout the entire galaxy, or if he thought it would be possible to turn them back on.

She breathed in the stillness, the sound loud in her ears as her brain tried to reconcile its new position, the absence of the Current.

And then she stepped toward Striker. He stood in the center of the platform, flapping his hands like he thought he could bring the Currents back through some kind of magic spell. Now that she was close, with no visions in the way, she could see the web of wires bursting out of the top of his helmet like spindly arms. Or hair, maybe. Each one had a sensor at the end. He looked like a combination of a porcupine and a kid playing robot.

They'd been making some assumptions about his level of desperation. Every once in a while, though, her assumptions turned out to be well founded. And Striker's desperation was obvious now as he grabbed one of the wires, pulling hard. A small image of a spaceship bubbled out of the end before vanishing.

The pictures needed more power to stay in focus. Currents, or wormholes. The illusions couldn't survive on their own. What reason could anyone have to create a machine like this?

But that didn't matter. Striker was done. The galaxy was safe. The end.

Sloane opened her comms to broadcast on every available channel. To make sure he heard what she had to tell him. "You're the one who's alone," she said.

Striker whipped around, sending the wires undulating in every direction. His teeth were bared behind the visor, a clump of reddish hair smeared across his forehead like a stain. "Don't you see?" he growled. "They are *coming* for us. Aliens. They've visited us before, and not with good intentions. They *will* come for us."

Why not bring it to the FAC, then? Why not partner with the Fleet to find a solution?

But Sloane was done asking why. She knew the answer. Striker wanted an empire. Defeating the aliens was only a piece of the puzzle, an excuse. He wanted to rule.

Seemed like an awful lot of work for one guy. But each to his own.

"If they do come," she said, "we'll face them together. Just not the way you envisioned it."

In one swift motion, Striker released his boots from the platform and launched himself through the vacuum toward Sloane.

He was lucky his aim was good, since he wasn't tethered. Sloane let him crash into her, keeping her own boots fully magnetized.

Striker lifted his elbow and smashed at her helmet with his elbow.

Sloane was ready for him. She let her head snap back, at the same time grabbing a fistful of the wires from the back of his head.

She didn't know how the weapon thing worked. Maybe it needed to be hooked to her helmet.

If it worked, then it worked. If not, well, Hilda and the others would have to tell her story.

In her mind, she imagined the Current. The healthiest version of it, the tropical road that connected them all in ways they might never understand. She imagined the waves swirling to life around Striker, the tug of the tides against his atmo suit, even the song that Gareth said he heard.

For a breath, she thought it wasn't working.

And then Striker grinned, releasing her helmet. "The Currents. I *won*."

Sloane demagnetized her right boot and kicked him in the stomach, letting go of the hallucination wires as she did. Striker thrashed for the back of her helmet, smacking it hard but missing his grip as he tumbled out and away from the platform. Sloane ducked, twisting awkwardly to watch as Striker went tumbling out into the vacuum. She couldn't see his face, but she preferred to imagine him screaming.

No more Striker. No more empire. No more hallucination weapons or planetary shields. They'd done it.

No more Currents, also. But hopefully that'd turn out to be a temporary problem.

When she tried to stand, though, her muscles didn't want to respond. She was breathing hard, watching Striker tumble out and away, his shadow growing fainter by the minute. She was breathing a little *too* hard, come to think of it. Little spots collected at the edges of her vision, a pretty pattern of light and darkness that was never a good sign.

Huh, she thought. *I think my air is leaking.*

And then the black turned blacker, and consciousness slipped away.

CHAPTER 30

GARETH RECOGNIZED the soft posture of an unconscious soldier in zero-G. When he used the tether to pull himself up onto the platform, he could see that though Sloane's right boot was still magnetized, there was a gap between her left boot and the platform. Her arms were wide and loose.

Striker was nowhere in sight.

Anchored by the tether, Gareth pushed himself through the zero-G, aiming directly for Sloane. He caught hold of her arm, pulling himself down so he could magnetize his boots.

Her air hookup had been detached. He replaced it, frantically calculating how many minutes had passed since he'd last heard a sound from her. It couldn't have been long. He pulled her toward him, taking her helmet between his hands and peering into her visor. Her eyes were closed, but he couldn't see much beyond the reflection of his own visor.

"Hilda," he said, keeping his voice as even as possible. "We need an extraction."

"Sure thing, Commander," she said. There was excited shouting in the background, and he frowned, pulling Sloane closer. "Nice work."

"I think we lost Striker," he said.

He couldn't bring himself to say the rest.

"No, Commander," Hilda said. "Sloane sent him on the float, and we've taken him into custody. He's a prisoner now."

Gareth wished he could feel relieved. He wished he could feel anything other than panic as Sloane floated in his arms, too still. Was it his imagination, or were the edges of her lips tinged with blue?

He brushed the side of her helmet, imagining he was touching her skin. "Come on," he said. "Wake up. We won, damn it. *You* won."

Without her, the Parse Galaxy would already be under CTF rule. Striker's rule. She'd stopped him. She'd finished it. She had to see the results. She *had* to.

And then she gasped, her eyes flying open. "Striker," she said, "he's— What's wrong?"

There was no way to wipe the tears out of his eyes, so he just let them flow. "You weren't breathing."

"Oh, that. Well, I'm breathing now. No worries."

He made himself smile. "None."

She set her hands on his arms, steadying herself. "So, Fortune, did I break the galaxy and get us stranded out here? Or do you think you can turn the Currents back on?"

Could he? What song should he even reach for, when there was no song in his ears? Asking the Current to shut off had been easy enough, though he had to admit to a sliver of surprise at the lack of protest from it. But he'd neglected to ask how to summon it again. He doubted he'd have understood its instructions, anyway.

Moneymaker was drawing nearer, Hilda clearly making a careful approach to the platform.

He tried to imagine the song, the winding melodies. He tried to hear the harmonies, weaving between them in dips and swells.

All this time, he'd been keeping a barrier in place. A wall, shoved firmly between his mind and the whispers, the songs that wanted to intrude. He'd *seen* them as intruders, too. Parasites, dangerous and impossible to explain.

But now... now, he knew what they were. They were, inexplicably, programmed to run on the power of human consciousness. Perhaps that made them more prone to errors. Or perhaps... perhaps those preserved consciousnesses were working together somehow. Holding one another accountable as they worked to operate the most important bit of technology in the galaxy.

Gareth let out a breath, while Sloane waited, clearly understanding she couldn't rush him. He closed his eyes. And then he tore down the wall, inviting the Current's song well and truly into his mind, inviting the whispers. Inviting all of it.

Because there'd been a piece of it within him all along, hadn't there? Ever since he'd plunged into that stasis field after Sands, it'd connected him with this technology in a way he wasn't sure he'd ever fully understand. But he didn't have to understand it. He just had to accept it.

Brick by brick, he crushed the wall to bits, allowing that piece of himself to filter through his own consciousness, to meet the empty space where the song belonged.

And it heard his call. Gently, the Currents faded back into being, as if they'd only been taking a quick break. Not a flash or a storm, but a quiet appearance, like someone twisting a dimmer switch back to full light.

They'd changed course, too, ever so slightly, an altered path that allowed *Moneymaker*—and the platform—to stay in normal space. Which would make it far more comfortable to reenter the Currents. He wondered if it'd done the same for any other ships that must've been in the Current when it dropped away, then decided that it probably had.

The song was back, too, like a background of chimes.

Thank you, he thought. The chimes muttered in response.

Sloane patted his arm, and he could see that she was smiling behind her visor as *Moneymaker* eased up alongside the platform.

Together, they limped into the airlock.

CHAPTER 31

MONEYMAKER'S KITCHEN was crowded again. But as Sloane made her way out of the infirmary—which she hadn't needed but had visited out of deference to Gareth, who'd looked like he might cry again if she refused—she had to admit that she kind of liked it this way.

No, not kind of. She *did* like it this way.

Hilda sat at the edge of the horseshoe-shaped booth in the galley, with Vin somehow miraculously tucked in beside her. Sloane could see their fingers laced together on Hilda's knee, and she narrowly kept herself from pumping her fist in celebration. Nothing like near-galactic annihilation to make two people realize they had the hots for each other. Or love. Whatever.

Brighton sat in the deepest end of the booth, eyeing Hilda and Vin warily, as if he feared they might change their minds and start fighting. Next to him, Alex and Ivy sat curled together like they never intended to let each other go.

And there was Gareth, waiting in her usual spot.

Yeah, she definitely liked the crowd. It was crowded with family, after all.

Sloane joined Gareth at the counter, and he smoothed her

hair away from her face, looking at her like he expected her to vanish into thin air or randomly stop breathing again. Which had totally been a one-time thing.

"I still don't understand how shaking makes money," Brighton was saying. Oh, good. The *Moneymaker* joke had come up again. The explanation was clearly still a question mark.

Sloane leaned into Gareth's side, breathing him in. "Shake your body," she said. "You know, you're hot. So you make money."

Ivy tilted her head. "So you're a prostitute. Licensed or unlicensed? I guess it doesn't matter. I think I understand the joke now."

"Not exactly." Sloane twisted to turn on her coffee machine, opening the cabinet to root through for a mug. If any moment called for coffee, it was this one.

"But if you make money shaking your body," Ivy said, "then you're a prostitute."

"Or a stripper," Brighton said.

Ivy nodded thoughtfully.

"I guess," Sloane said. "It's just—"

"It's a Milky Way thing," Hilda said.

Vin was looking at her like she was the best thing he'd ever seen, but Sloane made a mental note to corner him later and threaten him with a short walk out of the airlock if he did anything to hurt her.

"So I guess Striker's locked up?" Sloane asked.

"I stuck him in a storage cabinet," Brighton said. "Don't worry. I poked holes for breathing."

Sloane wasn't sure she'd have bothered. She definitely didn't like the idea of him on her ship. Wrinkling her nose, she flicked a spot of dirt out of the mug. Looked like the dish cycler might need maintenance soon. "You're nicer than I am. I'd have let him float. The Fleet's a goody-goody influence on us."

"True," Hilda said. "Should probably ditch them."

"Nah," Sloane said. "I like this one."

She gave Gareth a wink, which he returned, then lifted herself on tiptoes to see into the cabinet. Mugs, yes. Sugar dish, half full. Tea, way too much.

"So, now what?" Hilda asked. "We deliver Striker here to the nearest jail cell."

"We deliver him to Lostelle, I think. Seems like it's going to be the center of this new alliance thing Gareth's putting together."

Hilda shifted in her seat, watching as Sloane started removing boxes of tea from the cabinet. "You make it sound like a school project."

"Thank you for that," Gareth said.

"Calling it like I see it, Commander. All right, so we drop the loser on Lostelle. And then?"

Silence. Sloane figured they could rest for a week or seven before they needed to decide on their next move. On the other hand, saving the galaxy hadn't put many tokens in her pockets. They should probably find some paying work.

"Well, I'm getting back to work on wormholes," Alex said. "Escher's down there pulling out my old machines. Someone's going to need to drop us at the Hold."

Vin shrugged, like the only plan he had was to stick close to Hilda. Brighton mimicked the expression. *Moneymaker* was home; wherever it went, he'd go, too.

"I might have some ideas," Gareth said. "But maybe we can rest first."

Yes, Sloane had heard Candace's request. As Gareth's mother had no doubt intended her to. She wanted them to take over her super-secret spying organization or something. Might not be so bad, really. It'd keep them busy. As long as the stakes weren't galaxy level, it might be a fun gig.

Still, she couldn't help thinking that a nice, quiet delivery service might be the way to go.

Whatever she chose, she'd need to visit Elter first. Spend some time with Felicity, if her sister would allow it. Make up for how much of it she'd lost.

For now, Sloane replaced her mug into the cabinet and shut the door. She'd seen this day coming for a long time, and it was time to face the facts. "Would it be irresponsible to do a Milky Way wormhole first?"

"Why?" Brighton asked. "So they can explain your money-maker jokes?"

Sloane shook her head. "No. It's just, I'm out of coffee."

THE END

***

Thank you so much for spending so much time exploring the Parse Galaxy with me. Your support and enthusiasm for these books means the world to me!

─────

Sign up for my newsletter and keep reading with your free VIP Crew Library Collection! It's packed full of extras from the *Parse Galaxy*, the *League of Independent Operatives*, and *The Interstellar Trials*—with bonus stories, novellas, deleted scenes, and more!

Join now at KateSheeranSwed.com/Join-The-Crew

ALSO BY KATE SHEERAN SWED

Mastermind

Nemesis

Defender

For the most up-to-date information on my books, visit
KateSheeranSwed.com.

ABOUT THE AUTHOR

Kate Sheeran Swed loves hot chocolate, plastic dinosaurs, and airplane tickets. She has trekked along the Inca Trail to Macchu Picchu, hiked on the Mýrdalsjökull glacier in Iceland, and climbed the ruins of Masada to watch the sunrise over the Dead Sea. Kate currently lives in New York's capital region with her husband and two kids, plus a pair of cats who were named after movie dogs (Benji and Beethoven). She holds an MFA in Fiction from Pacific University.

You can find more of Kate's work, and pick up a free novella, at katesheeranswed.com.

facebook.com/katesheeranswed

instagram.com/katesheeranswed

youtube.com/@katesheeranswed

www.ingramcontent.com/pod-product-compliance
Lightning Source LLC
Chambersburg PA
CBHW020839260626
47169CB00003B/1056